More Praise for
Periphylla, and Other Deep Ocean Attractions

A fever-hot exhalation of wonder. In these stories, aquariums hold leviathans, amoeba people burst through fake human skins, bruises ache from past lives, and the dead return as pigs. Heady, blistering, and tender as a wound.

—**Micah Dean Hicks,** author of *Break the Bodies, Haunt the Bones*

Periphylla, and Other Deep Ocean Attractions is an intense read, it is teeming with life in so many forms: sea creatures (obviously) but also yak, pigs, reptiles, peacocks, snails, spiders, even single-celled organisms. Each story has its own strong voice, and in each story, Ashley manages to create a separate, memorable world. More often than not, the boundaries between human and animal life become permeable, if not invisible."

—**Annette C. Boehm,** author of *The Apidictor Tapes*

PERIPHYLLA AND OTHER DEEP OCEAN. ATTRACTIONS

Runner-Up for the Press 53 Award for Short Fiction

GARRETT ASHLEY

Press 53

Winston-Salem

Press 53, LLC
PO Box 30314
Winston-Salem, NC 27301

First Edition

Cover design by Claire V. Foxx

Cover art: "Red Octopus with tentacles" by NaDo_Krasivo,
licensed with permission through Adobe Stock.

Library of Congress Control Number
2024935470

ISBN 978-19-50413-76-8

Faye

CONTENTS

PERIPHYLLA, AND OTHER DEEP OCEAN ATTRACTIONS

On either side of the hallway leading down the bathyal zone grow a myriad of midnight corals: pink boas curling into fuzzy star-shaped patterns, dandelion blues like fleshy honeysuckles bunched in a rod. Then there are multicolored tunicates of all different shapes: the predatory ghost, a translucent balloon-esque creature sitting on string and glowing in a soft light, its flapping sack closing on whatever drifts into its mouth; bluebells, ribbed and electrical, reminiscent of the colon or fancy condoms; sea squirts, veiny, embarrassing, bloated, gold-mouthed. And there are the anemones, standard, except for the flytrap anemone, which retains the will to travel while others remain sessile.

The flytrap anemone behaves similarly to the Venus flytrap. She waits for living prey to brush across her rubber tendrils before clamping her coconut-shaped beak. She can be very beautiful and simultaneously deadly. She wants feverishly to escape the dreaded nothingness of her existence. The movement of flytrap anemones is entirely dependent on their shape and size; a starfish might invade the territory of an anemone (the Deep-Sea Atrium has plenty of scavengers), and the anemone, whose body is usually shaped in such a way that it has trouble plucking things from the ground, might leap up and shuffle away through the water (as though pulsating on air) before landing in a more welcoming spot. Which may only be the case for flytrap anemones with fatter necks; a thin, twig-like neck can prevent the anemone from taking flight, but the organism might still be able to develop motor functions at the base of its smooth torso or even grow leathery fingers to help it crawl away. The less mobile flytraps have been known to jump on the backs of vulnerable crustaceans that, once beneath the weight of the relatively cumbersome flytrap anemone, are unable to wiggle it away.

As you go past the coral chamber and I perform my last bit about the aquarium and safety and I fix your head with the blue phosphorescent headband, you'll begin your descent along a plaster replica of the continental slope, where your head clogs with the tanks' secondhand pressurization and where it gets so dark you'll not be able to recognize another face for the rest of the tour. And I'll begin to develop the photos of guests standing in the maw of a life-sized model of Leviathan (being eaten, swallowed—the beginning of their descent), their children's faces molded to horror. Most people don't buy the prints, but they look anyway, at how frightened they had been, then laugh; I smile and watch them go.

I would prefer to write about my life at the Deep-Sea Atrium. But in order to help confront the issues of my childhood, Tia suggested I write about my problem with thieving, instead. I told her I don't have a problem with thieving. I have a problem with being a college dropout. I have a problem with the lonely-necked zebra fish getting too thin and unattractive to the guests, with the tentacles of vampiric squid losing their patented bioluminescence. I have a problem with reintroducing myself at the end of the day to television flashes, dumb jokes, the people above us stomping, Tia's food, her tastes in music, her papers on the floor, her clothes on the floor, sometimes Tia on the floor stretching, giving me that look, like where have you been?—what are we doing? I have a problem with being told I've not done anything with my life, that I could do something with my life if I wanted to because I'm interesting and smart, when in fact I've felt happy with my job situation for quite some time.

There have been a few incidents of thieving. A few pieces of jewelry left in bathrooms, purses in corners unreported, useless pieces of junk I've snagged out of shopping bags, but it's not an ongoing thing, and it's never anything very substantial. And I don't, regardless of what my partner thinks, relate thieving metaphorically to anything going on in my life, you know, my *life-life*.

Anglers are particularly strange for their not altogether unheard-of mating rituals. The thumb-sized males latch onto the side of a female angler's body, then become slowly absorbed over time: their pin-sized teeth melt the outer surface of the female, grafting his mouth to her skin, and soon the thumb-sized male's torso is able to absorb nutrients from the female, while she extracts sperm as per necessary. This seems to be a random occurrence in evolution that her body cannot control. Maybe she feels bad about this. Maybe, when she scrapes against a rock and feels the tumorous bulge, she is reminded of something sad. A hospital bill, old roommates. Straight days. After a while, after the male's eyes dissolve, his lungs, his snout, his brains all disappear, and the only thing that'll be left are testicles. The discolored mole that is left behind will only vaguely resemble a once sentient creature. This is all information probably everyone knows by now, but what's interesting is why anglers do it, why it's necessary for their survival: when you live so far in the dark, attachment becomes essential. And for fish, especially the angler, practical relationships cannot exist. It isn't difficult to think occasionally of a girl, for instance, who was there for you when your college boyfriend broke up with you shortly after a rough miscarriage. And also, it isn't difficult to feel compelled to stay with someone because you feel sorry for them.

Such is the way of the horned lantern breed of angler, which is the species we have in containment. She trembles through the water with her sperm-filled mole hanging off the top of her head adjacent to the bioluminescent rod and lure, which droops in the middle as a result of nerve damage. She hangs in the water beneath a timid yellow light. Extendable jaw and elastic stomach full of shrimp and other tank debris. The tank is not very high but extends far back into the exhibit into a solid darkness. A darkness you can feel, of which you can say to yourself, upon entering the room, *There is something there in the shadows.* This particular angler isn't very good at hiding her mole; we don't even know that she cares. It's especially striking once you learn what the mole is, what it was, how lonely things must be as a result of this non-relationship.

I wonder about what Kelsey does with the eggs when they're laid; the exhibit isn't big enough to accurately represent such a vast expanse of ocean and would thus render the mating habits of these particular fish useless, that is, if it turns out to be too easy to find a mate. I'm curious, then, if the anglers will find a way to adapt to the convenience of living within such close proximity. Also, I've decided this is what it's like to live in a house with another person; they get too close to you at night on the couch when you want to unwind, hold on to you with their dull, wide teeth, talk about all the times they thought about you through the day and how sometimes they just wish they could carry you in their pocket or wear you on their back for comfort. . . .

The man I adjusted the headband to this morning had a big sebum-filled nose with holes you could stick a cork into. His blackheads glowed in the purple light. Purple eyes, and age lines above his eyes. I bumped into him upon entry, and his wallet flopped onto the floor, and I took it without even looking around. I thought to myself, *Well, if anyone sees me taking this wallet, I'll say I intended to turn it in to the front desk.* The wallet is thick with receipts, coupons, singles, expired debit cards, three old licenses with the same picture of a younger self, a folded-up bank statement, a sliver of paper with numbers on it, probably a banking or routing number. The man came back later and said he'd lost his wallet, and the box-office girl and I spent thirty minutes looking for it. I convinced myself that the wallet had actually been lost. On the way home, I felt it in my back pocket. I took out the singles and threw the rest out the window.

The dull plopping sound of the dead whale reverberated through the atrium up to the coral exhibit. I adjusted a blue headband to a young woman with a round scar on her cheekbone. The current dead whale on exhibit is key in the life cycle of several deep-ocean species and for a better understanding of what happens to the large mesopelagic creatures when they die. The carcass of a whale is placed in the first tank high above the primary tank, which is then slowly pressurized in order to simulate a descent into the dark ocean, as the carcass would weave and bob until it hit bottom; then as the pressurization of the first chamber matches the primary chamber, the one we see here, the door opens and the whale plops in, midsection first, then the head, then the stiff tail. The sound attracts a multitude of scavengers from adjacent tanks: hagfish and crabs, starfish and small crustaceans, which over time feast on the whale's carcass until there's nothing left but bone. The main chamber is a whale graveyard of bone and deteriorating flesh. The hagfish tie themselves up for leverage and pop pieces of fat off the carcass and look like little tentacles undulating in an ocean current. Crabs build mountains of one another, create divisions, negotiate the terrain of a thousand bodies, have reunions, pray, form alliances, fuck, and fend off starfish and shrimp from their crab-bodied fortresses. Occasionally someone turns a knob and the lights brighten, allowing us to see the whale in full. The hagfish are the most frightening part of the show. Their ribbonesque bodies, when they latch onto the whale with their teeth, look like plumes of lost alien juice.

While barely visible in the purple light, the whale seems to leak some black, essential material.

I don't know what we learn from the image of a devoured whale.

This is the most natural way to feed our scavengers. Cameron claims we can benefit from this, too; he came through the other day and noticed me. "It's pretty cool how they don't seem to mind one another," he said, referring to the scavengers. "I mean the hagfish and the crabs. The crabs don't like starfish though. Hmm. But you know." I know? I like rock music and I like burritos. I like insects and I like fish. I like the dark and I like sleeping. I'm interested in the way animals communicate with one another across species, dogs and cats especially, how some species are inherently more comfortable intermixing than others. Territory, somehow, doesn't translate across all boarders. Or maybe it does? "Yeah, it's pretty cool," I said. Then Cameron left to go do whatever Cameron does.

In the break room I found Erica's ID card under one of the tables. This gave me the idea to go through her locker since I was alone and Erica didn't have a lock. Inside sat a child-sized backpack with a clear plastic front pocket containing crayons, waxy crumbs, mechanical pencils, and scraps of notebook paper. A pair of Sony headphones hung from the pocket at the top. The walls rumbled, which meant they were feeding sharks to Leviathan. Erica also had a pair of shoes in the locker, a bike lock and cord, and a Kodak FZ41 digital camera. I stuffed the camera in my back pocket and was working on the headphones when the cord became hung in a tiny rubber hole at the top of her backpack, and I was afraid of being caught, so I decided the camera was enough. Leviathan grumbled. The ceiling vibrated, dust stirred, lights blinked, a roach shot out of a hole in the wall, and I stepped back before it came near me.

The jellyfish exhibit holds a special significance for me because the big helmet jellies are named after me by Cameron, whose job is to curate them. The tank, a seven-story obelisk capable of producing pressures of up to a ton per square centimeter, allows for a simulated ascent to the top of the obelisk, where the pink-bodied periphylla are enveloped in clouds of plankton. The Catherines' coronal openings extend vaginally to capture pockets of plankton. Visitors may climb a staircase in order to watch the collected Catherines feed: bell-shaped, helmet-shaped, brainless sock hats, floating globs of disinterested nervous system. Most are bioluminescent around the lip, and as the current whips them around the tank, they glow a sort of estranged blue color.

What's strange about the helmet jellyfish is that its pink and often red color is not only very beautiful to look at, especially when the creatures grow to their full potential (the size of a car engine, the size of a human torso), but is also potentially very dangerous for the creature due to its lack of ferrochelatase, an enzyme that produces a ferrous iron in the pigment porphyrin. I didn't know, for instance, that a Catherine could develop a rash if it swims too far to the surface; for this reason, the Catherines stay in the deepest parts of the ocean. Not that periphylla know one way or the other about the shallows, about the world above. They're jellyfish, and they don't know anything. Except it's sad that they have all this color and nothing to do with it, really, but scare off predators.

Cameron calls the periphylla "Catherines" not because I'm disinterested; the opposite is true. I've tried so hard to give him the impression that I know what I'm talking about. We've discussed the mating habits of whales, for instance. And I've talked extensively about my time at the entomology exhibit, where I was the bug girl—shining blue lights on scorpions, letting fat centipedes crawl on my arm and across the guests' hands. When Cameron compares me to a jellyfish, it's because I spend too much of my off time in the atrium, like I have no interest in ever leaving.

I think Cameron feels the same about me—good? possibly attracted?—but I can't be sure of anything.

During the day he keeps an eye on the periphylla obelisk (there are forty-seven large Catherines in all). When the periphylla finish gorging on plankton, he switches the circulators off, and they slalom to the bottom like snowflakes. Then Cameron plops down into the tank to clear the glass of bacteria and feces. He does this after closing, and I might watch every now and then and think about all the things I know about Cameron: That he's from Pascagoula, for one—not very informative. Cameron rides a bicycle to work. Cameron has never been on a train, and he's never been west of the Mississippi River. Cameron knows more about breeding jellyfish than he knows about women, he claims, and he's never seen a human child equal in charm to a polyp or as abundant in personality as the eggs of a periphylla. He says when they're freshly strewn, the eggs remind him of stars.

Erica changed into the alternate pair of shoes at her locker. She noticed the headphones were poking up from her backpack and shoved them back down. She slammed the locker and left, made no comment about the camera that was currently in my front pocket (I was sitting, eating a chicken wrap). When I got home I put the camera in the plastic tub under the bed. I worried about what might be on the camera (pictures of Erica, her life, etc.), what might happen if Tia found the camera and looked through it because . . . having these talks with Tia—they make me feel . . .

Sepphoris is outgrowing the gutted-out back end of the Soviet Series-VI M-class submarine. She's the offspring a giant and colossal squid, genetically altered to be equal in size to a blue whale; her mantle is as long and fat as a school bus, her eyes like wrecking balls. Sepphoris is extremely difficult to care for, unlike Leviathan, who's also large but actually quite gentle (depression). Anthony's back, for instance, has scars from the chitinous rings of her suckers, and he can no longer go into the tank alone. Anthony has done television interviews regarding the dangers of working with Sepphoris. There have been numerous television specials on Sepphoris. Anthony, to some extent, is a hero at the atrium, and this adds to his general attraction (Anthony has long hair, bored eyes, silver teeth from a surfing accident some years before). It turns out to be no small ordeal, freeing Sepphoris from her M-class. For a while we thought she'd just wear the submarine like a skirt. She picked up the hull slightly and lifted up a few yards before sagging back down with a plunk. Outside, they did a mural of the goliath squid wrapped in submarine parts. Fliers portray Sepphoris as a much larger beast actually overtaking a submarine. I imagine she stays in the submarine to avoid light. She's blind in one eye, and Anthony says having vision on only one side of her body has made her aggressive. The blind eye is reminiscent of an old television screen tuned to static. If Sepphoris ever kills Anthony, it'll be because she couldn't see him coming, because he made the mistake of contacting her from the wrong side, of looking too long into her silvery eye, his frightened body shaking to produce threatening vibrations.

It means a lot that you care. I don't mind that you care. I think sometimes about when I was going through my house-cleaning phase and I cut my middle finger in the blender. The blades wouldn't come out. We went to a store for Band-Aids, and blood dripped everywhere. You've never been embarrassed by me. Which makes me feel awful about the times I've pretended I didn't know you as well as I know you; for example, you have a loud voice, and the more interesting a story is to you, the louder you tell it, the more you want other people to know how interesting your life is. And also, for example, there was this one time at a tennis court when a dog jumped on a tiny bird, and you lost your mind. I was embarrassed by that: Is that such a bad thing, that I associate your entirety with these tinier moments? Is it a bad thing to want to hide myself, to grumble when I don't have an answer?

◆ ◆ ◆

Let me talk about sawtooth eels. They float upright, their faces always looking in the direction of the sun. In the wild they are lonely creatures; they'll wait ages for trash (a dead fish, crumbs from a larger predator's meal) to drop down close enough for them to engorge. And they know how to engorge: a sawtooth eel can consume more than ten times its own weight, fitting its meal into a soft-bodied sack hanging under it like an old man's paunch. The largest known meal consumed by the four-foot-long, belt-sized sawtooth eel was a bottlenose dolphin. It isn't known how the eel came to be here on earth, how long he plans to stay, where he'll be spotted next in the vast emptiness of the Pacific Ocean.

While they are lonely in the wild, in the atrium they float in a circle near one another like a monument. The lights are adjusted so guests will feel a sense of unease as they strain to see into the tank: Those things, hey, what is that? Are those alive? They have a variety of faces: fat-jawed and mangled, slender and pin-like. The eels, not the guests. I imagine what it's like to float there and wait for something to drop into their mouths. I imagine that's the only thing they think about, all day. They literally have nothing else to do but wait. If one eel needs to shit, it shits; its companions don't even bat an eye, they're so amazingly focused.

Cameron: If he reads this, would he believe I'm not as stupid as he thinks? Some days I see him handling manta rays in the coral exhibit; they paddle around in a circle and come up to him like hungry stray cats when he whistles. Sometimes I see him pulverizing canned chicken into sludge for feed. When I go home, Tia asks why I smell like the ocean; I don't work at the ocean, only a simulation of the ocean. What is it that I smell like?

I wait, and I wait, and I wait.

Tia has bad posture: she slumps when she comes in, sighs heavily, waves her hand at the cat. She starts every sentence with a loud huff. She finds the camera because

I'd taken it out to look through the memory card and forgot to put it back. So my explanation consists of two lies—one, that it'd belonged to no one, had been in a random unmarked locker for months, unclaimed, and also that after asking around whether it belonged to anyone, Erica herself gave me a memory card to go along with it, just in case the camera didn't already have one, which she'd also forgotten to wipe clean. Here we are, the two of us, waiting for the tension to clear up, tension that inks from our chests, that grabs and pops, a sort of knowing, a sort of darkness. The camera could mean anything: lies I've told, stories, things I've found important in the past but didn't have the strength to share. Aren't we supposed to be there for one another? To talk about when we're feeling claustrophobic, when the air in the room is too thick, when our living is too small? How do I say, for instance, that I would prefer to talk about something meaningful at dinner instead of watching television? How do I say, for instance, that my original intention was to move in with someone I cared for rather than someone I found convenient? How do I tell her that there are a million people in the city looking for a roommate, that I could make it if I wanted to, no strings attached, without the additional worry of *you could do so much better*?

There are no good aquariums. Traveling into the heart of the Deep-Sea Atrium is not like a cave tour where there are lights strung up on the wall and a guide to lead you along. Nor is it for the faint of heart, at least not the faint heart that is also afraid of dark, enclosed spaces. As you begin to encounter other guests, you sense a sort of change in your eyesight. This woman becomes a shadow of her old self, the self you noticed in the lobby. Phosphorescent headbands become more luminescent. This man who claims he lost his wallet seems crazy, sounds needled. You think about an argument you've had with your mother about jewelry she's gotten rid of without your permission. Or you think about how silly it was that you got upset that your brother-in-law was looking at photos of short-haired girls on Facebook, right in front of your sister. You lose a part of yourself, encased in the ocean; maybe you'll trip over one another at first as you try to find the little orbs of light guiding your way along the floor; maybe I'll remember Tia one day, remember that what I have outside is a life and that there are people who want to see me and have mindless conversations. But for now. What we have of one another are glowing blue headbands, which keep the guests from bumping into one another. They'll be able to study the creatures for as long as they want. And eventually they exit, one at a time, up to the main lobby, where I'll offer them their photographs before releasing them back into the real world. Part of the excitement, I like to think, is finding a way out.

ONCE WAS A YAK

My nine-year-old, Joy, has finally taken an interest in my disabilities. I was born with a small hand, and one of my ears is shriveled to the shape of a peanut. Joy knows there is something different about me. I catch her looking all the time. We're in the backyard, spreading mulch over the flower bed. She carries sticks from one side of the yard to the other. The cat that lives under the steps follows her around, its tail curled and happy. I understand Joy's curiosity is supposed to be normal. But she's also frightened. Not of me but of something in herself. Something she hasn't grown into yet. She has my crooked nose, my brown eyes, my lanky, miniscule figure, but she has not inherited anything else. She will see, one day, that her worry over deformities is a waste of time and love and energy.

Joy's fear of me stems from my basic incompetence as a father. Nothing special or interesting to say about that, other than I have not always been the best, and so perhaps she associates my appearance with badness. Her mother, Laurie, divorced me a couple years ago, and for a while I was extremely depressed and difficult to be around. When Joy came over I floated around the house, uncaring, doing only what was necessary to keep her entertained.

My regular doctor asks about my past life as a yak. I was eating grains in my sleep, the night before. Where do I see myself going now? She thinks that my incompetence as a father stems from issues with self-image. Mostly this comes as a result of my interactions with children: they look at me, ask questions, and I hear the adults shushing, begging them not to be so embarrassing.

I've even heard Joy ask her mother why I look the way I do. Joy looks at herself in the mirror, pulls at her well-formed ear, rubs her hands together, cries, squeezes ribbons, bedsheets, shirttails, things she can ball into little fists. I remember when I was little, my mother wouldn't allow me to look at people who were disabled. I remember a one-armed man coming to our door with a package. My mother held me. The man was standing there, his one hand hanging down next to his pocket, the nub of his other pointed toward me. The skin at the elbow was tucked in like a belly button.

I have this idea that Joy fears growing up and being something less than human, and when she cries, I imagine it is only for fear of me, and I want to cry, that part of me that loves my daughter, but I tell myself that crying is for weak people, so that's not what I need to do at all.

I earnestly believe in my memory of being a yak. And I find the image of the yak to be useful in coming to terms with the way things are now. I practice telling my story to the cat: "Once, a long time ago, I was a big, bull-shouldered yak, like the ones who live in the snow between the southern border of Russia and Mongolia. Hair curled into my eyes. I had horns like a mustache, and a bulbous sore spot had begun to grow on my back. These days if I'm sitting in a chair and rub against my birthmark, I'll remember that the man with a small arm never saddled me again, that I was always in pain, and that there had been no way to end my suffering."

My ex-wife was once a snail. Laurie was also once a bank manager who was shot in the jaw. When we met she told me about her birthmark, that she'd been living in New Orleans and had been shot in the jaw outside a jewelry store.

She'd had a wife who didn't love her anymore. She'd had a balcony garden and played the piano. When she was shot in the jaw, she lay on the street a while before dying. She thought about all the things wrong with her life and wished she had done things differently.

When she was a kid, Laurie surprised her parents by playing a song on their piano without ever having taken a single lesson. How wonderful, her parents must have thought, that we forget some memories, and the ones that come to us are always sort of fleeting things with no connection to anything. And how sad, too, that not everyone is able to access those memories.

Laurie says she's written it all down. She's taken an interest in psychoanalytical theory. And writing is a sort of therapy for her, even when the subject is hard. Sometimes she can only remember the bad things. And then there are times when she remembers something good, but she doesn't know what life it's coming from, whether tangible or dream, Laurie or someone else entirely.

She says she's proud of me for coming to her for help. Laurie is proud that I see the things our daughter sees, finally—my ear and hand, the little shakes I get, the way my voice drops when I'm tired—they're not so much obstacles, "Like, they're really just platforms. You stand on them. They're not obstacles," she says. "You just need to talk to Joy. That's, like, all you have to do." And really, there comes that warm feeling, like things can get better if I start to see things more like Laurie. My ex-wife has never been so helpful to me before, and I just get this really good feeling about things, which I can't explain.

I didn't remember being a yak until the second grade. I started getting headaches. I recalled words in a language I'd never heard before. These words were associated with the actions "behave" and "eat." I had weight on my back. The man walked up and held a bowl of grain under my nose. He put the bowl down on the rocks and beat me with his whip. When I wouldn't eat the grain, my body trembling under the weight of the man's cargo and the slap of the whip, he sat on a rock and cried into his knees. His small arm rocked in the wind like a hammock.

"Once I was a yak. Once upon a time, I was a yak." I try to figure out the best way to tell it. When I pick Joy up from school one day, I try to tell it. Except she has so much to say on the way home. A new kid in a wheelchair visited her class today. Lunch consisted of turkey meatloaf and a bowl of steamed carrots. Her friend Laney had a blank look throughout recess. Laney had an emotional breakdown this morning, said she was losing sleep and her parents wouldn't do anything about the things creeping into her room at night, bugs, squirrels, etc. Laney needs a cat, something like the cat who lives under our porch steps. Joy talks until she falls asleep in the backseat. I want to tell Joy that I know Laney very well. Joy doesn't know, for instance, that Laney's living conditions are substantially different than her own, that cockroaches and lizards by the dozens are always within an arm's reach. I know Laney's parents, and I know how people live, how they allow their children to live, the words they say, and the things they do.

I don't know how to make the story of my past life interesting or relevant when there are other people with more important things to say. I don't recall what happened to the man with the tiny arm or why he cried when I wouldn't eat. If I don't know what happened, then I should not try to give him a story. I keep telling myself that I don't know anything about anything about anything.

I'm on the phone with Joy. She's crying about something, and then she just comes right out and says it. I've ruined her birthday. I ask kindly to speak to her mother. Apparently, Laurie told her this morning that I wouldn't be picking her up this weekend for her birthday because I would be working. Things were going well at first, but it looks like Laurie never meant any of what she'd said about being proud, and she is still out to get me for some reason. I tell Laurie I'm not working—I haven't gone in on a weekend for more than a year.

I'm shaken up by this. Of course, nobody likes disappointing their kids.

"I just thought it'd be more convenient if you just do her birthday separate."

"Separate from what?" I say. "Separate from her birthday?"

Afterward I go to the bathroom and take six ibuprofens. Then I retrieve the cat from under the steps and hold him until he claws away from me. Then I think whatever, I'll just go see Joy on her birthday anyway.

Before I get out of the car, I look at myself in the reflection in the passenger-side window and wonder if Laurie still finds me attractive. Then I remember I'm supposed to be angry, and also I'm divorced, and she's married to Bill. The problem with sustaining anger is sometimes I find myself in positions where I need to feel angry, but my anger turns out to be more for show. I'm angry when I want to get my way. Or when I need to be angry, when it's socially acceptable that I become angered. But there's hardly ever any feeling there, except the feeling of letting something out.

The new husband, Bill, a state department employee and body builder, finds me on the back porch, petting their dog. He asks how I'm doing. I find him difficult to face since he's carrying a handful of balloons. I tell him I'm fine. He asks where Joy has gotten off to. I tell him she went around the side of the house with a water hose. He asks how I'm doing again, like he hadn't heard my answer before. I tell him I'll bust him in the nose if he doesn't get back inside. To which he rattles his left hand around in his pockets and says, "Yeah, okay, Charles, that's fine by me."

"Once upon a time I was a lion." It would be better to make myself into a more interesting creature, but that would be lying, and I don't want to lie to Joy. I also need to find a way to make the story happy.

She won't understand the problem of adulthood—the man crying, for instance, or the fact I had been rendered useless by the sore on my back.

Joy has a dream sometimes that she lives in Nepal. She says they were hit by an earthquake recently. She has a birthmark on the back of her neck, below the hairline, where the bones were shattered. She says she wishes she were prettier, like the Nepalese.

She gets angry when I tell her she's pretty just the way she is.

Joy says something in Nepalese. I ask her where she learned that from, and she tells me she's known it all along, and then she speaks Nepalese for a week, and thus the communication issues arise, and just like that, she starts to grow out of it, like the whole Nepalese thing is just a phase.

"I thought you were never coming back," I say.

"I've been right here," she says.

"Once upon a time there was a yak that had a sore spot on its back. Its master was a poor farmer from—" But I'm thinking that maybe the unintentional rhyme makes the story less than interesting.

And it's not that I don't think this is a good idea—it's that I don't have the energy to recall any of this. I rely on my dreams to carry the narrative forward. I have no creative prowess, and if I could add warfare and disease and famine to the history of my past life, I would do so in a heartbeat. But my daughter sees right through me.

"You're like a knot on a log," she says.

"This is why there are children's books."

"Do you want a blanket?"

"I'm not cold," I say.

"Are you hungry?"

"I just want you to go to sleep," I say.

Bill has signed Joy up for piano lessons, so today I'm signing her up for karate. I plan on signing myself up as well, but I need a day or two to think about whether I'd be good for this sort of thing. I might have to fight a young kid. If a young person beats me in a fight, then I'll lose Joy's respect. If I beat a young person in a fight, I might also lose her respect. I really don't know if it's a good idea, signing her up for karate. From what I understand, karate is a purely disciplinary activity, but that could be any sport. If I wanted to play golf, it might be good if I had better discipline and a fully functional hand. Karate also comes off as too aggressive for a nine-year-old, which might be a problem, but I can't shy away from violence, considering that the world is a violent place and that we all have animals within us dictating what we do, the things we say. I have this idea in my head, at least, that karate will carry greater metaphorical significance than piano lessons.

What I remember, occasionally: big hides, glazed fur, stunted goats, crooked knees, frosted stones, frosted beards, matted hair, rotted teeth, broken noses, brittle grass, three fish hanging from strings, hardened mud, white feathers with spots of blood, a tiny chicken running into a bush, a tanning rack, a hot piece of ash against my rear, a broken wheel, an octagonal banner, rainclouds, a hill cut into the shape of a crow, baskets piled to the ceiling, mice huddled in a wooden bowl.

When I'm worried about something, I fold the pillow around my face at night. I dream of goats. There's one goat that limps around on its knees. I think I may be repressing some childhood memory. If my mother was around, I'd ask if I ever got bullied or whether we ever had a goat or whether I might have lived among goats. I might have also been a goat, at some point, with a limp. It's possible I'm destined to belong to a species of maimed, malformed animals.

Bill calls. He wants to know why I signed Joy up for karate lessons on Thursday afternoons. The time's sort of inconvenient, he says. "Why couldn't you have done it on weekends?"

I tell Bill, "You can take her there after school, and I can pick her up and drive her back to your place. It's not a big deal."

To which Bill replies, "I just wish you'd have talked to one of us about it. Karate's kind of violent, you know."

To which I respond, "You sound like a whale's dick when you get an attitude with me."

Bill, kind of whale's dick-like, tells me I can stick it up my ass, by which he means a big fucking dildo, and I tell Bill the only thing that's getting shoved up my ass is the ugly curtain rod they gave me when they changed around their living room. Bill stutters, says he hopes I break it off in my ass. "Good," I tell him and hang up.

I get Joy on Saturday. She has karate next Thursday and she's already nervous about it. She's started picking at her nails. She asks me why I signed her up for karate when I could have just taken her somewhere to hang out. We could have gone fishing. We could have gone bowling. "You can bowl with one hand," she says. Then she accuses me of just needing to get a babysitter for the weekend. "Is that what this is? You're trying to dump me off on the karate instructor?"

"I'm taking karate with you," I say.

"How are you going to do karate anyway?"

"Just like the rest of you."

"You're just trying to dump me off."

I ask where she learned all this from. I never use the word "dump" in front of her. I think it must have been Laurie, accusing me of washing my soul of everything and everyone. The reason we divorced, I think, is because I never wanted a family. Or she never wanted a family. It was one of us. Joy doesn't know how adults think yet. She doesn't know the complications involved with figuring out who has broken what, who is responsible for loving the children more.

"I'm just trying to be better with people," I say.

She mutters some response that I don't quite hear. I think about what I've said—the thing about being better with people. I don't know how true it is or why it was something I needed to say to a nine-year-old. I'm ashamed of certain things, yes, but it isn't entirely clear to me whether that's the thing I'm trying to change in my life. That would mean—wouldn't it?—that all my effort lately with Joy isn't about Joy at all but for my own benefit. I want to believe that I do things for the love of others, and that's a question I don't want to ask: whether I am selfish or whether, one day, when I'm gone, there will be anything pleasant to remember about me.

This is one way to feel closer to Joy. We sit on the floor together eating pizza. We have plans to camp in the back-yard tonight, like people say they do with their children.

Part of it is I need to forget about Bill, the trouble I must be causing him and Laurie, and this idea I have in my head about the damage I could potentially do to Joy. All this business of trying to win my daughter's admiration takes a deep psychological toll on me.

One way I try to bond with my daughter is we talk about our past lives. I imagine sitting in the dark under the moonlight with my daughter like they do in movies, talking all night about our other lives, a rush of excitement welling in us.

But Joy, as always, treats her memory like any other memory. She says she lived in a rock with a dimple on it. She had a wife with a forked tongue. She describes the rest to me like something from a dream, something she knows very little about and has thus been forced to improvise the meaning of.

I tell her once I was a yak.

"What's a yak?" she asks.

"You've never heard of a yak? Well, a yak is—big, and they're like cows—and they live where it's cold." And like clockwork I run out of things to say about yaks.

Since I don't have anything better to do, during the week I try to improvise more stories about being a yak. I write it all down as I go, like Laurie told me to do.

Once I was a yak, and the owner's green and gray hill was attacked by Mongol warriors, and it was up to me and my fellow yak brethren to defend the owner's family.

Another time when I was a yak, we yak were taken by a feudal warlord who wished to collect and sell our hides.

Once when I was a yak, a mysterious beast started devouring all our sheep. After investigating the deaths, I followed my leads to a cavern in the hills where a family of tigers slept, the bones of sheep stacked to the ceiling.

I don't know very much about Mongolia. I look it up and realize how difficult it will be to tell a full story without getting anything wrong. For instance, I have no idea if there are tigers in Mongolia. I vaguely recall a problem with tigers. It's possible that tigers migrate from Siberia, where there are Siberian tigers. Not that Joy would know the difference.

The story about the yak is, as far as I know, not about anything. And it's not always super depressing. Some-times the small-armed man put his estranged son in a playful headlock, snow building up on the roof above them. I was also very happy, sometimes, as a yak. I don't remember a time, for instance, when I ever thought things could be much better. I ate grass all day, kept warm, and slobbered. One would assume I fucked other yaks too.

Or maybe I didn't fuck other yaks. My grandfather, who had a small cattle farm, would only ever have one bull in a field of twenty or thirty cows. So assuming the practice of bull segregation is traditional, and has been so for many centuries, I might never have fucked another yak and might even have been raised for slaughter, which I can't even be sure is a traditional practice of the Mongolian people. More likely I just carried stuff on my back and ate grass and slobbered.

One thing I do remember for certain is being packed at times into groups of twenty or thirty yaks, with no way to turn my head. Then the man would walk among us, searching our teeth for imperfections. My memory of being packed in a group like this reminds me of the value of friendship and the occasional longing for solitude.

When I went off from the herd, far enough away to feel like I was the only yak in the world, I was taunted, beaten, returned. There were boundaries I was never meant to cross. The man with the short arm wanted never to lose me, I suppose, and I can't blame him for that.

There were times as a yak, I imagine, it is possible I felt overwhelmed, overused.

I'm sitting alone with Laurie, who has agreed to psychoanalyze me. She tells me the man with the small arm might come to represent my fear of disability.

She says I should start looking at my past experiences as dreams rather than events in order to better address the issues I have in the present.

Things in real life, historical events, do not, should not, be made representations of other events.

Laurie has an iguana in a cage, which she talks to when Bill and Joy are gone. She pulls it out of the cage and tells me to hold it.

"Stick your tongue out," she says.

The iguana sticks its tongue out.

"Raise your left foot."

The iguana does as she asks.

"Give me a kiss."

It gives her a small, cold-lipped kiss.

She tells me the iguana was an old boyfriend. Then laughs and shakes her head, drops the iguana back in its cage. There's no way she could know something like that. "How is the karate going?" she asks, but I have a feeling that no matter what I tell her, she's only half listening.

Rather than tell Joy about the yak, I try to explain my hand and the way I've experienced having a twisted, shrunken ear. "You can look at it. I don't care. You've never asked about my ear before, so I thought your mother had told you it was rude or something. It's okay to want to look. If you didn't look you wouldn't be normal. It's not just because you're a little girl that you want to look.

Grown-ass adults look at my face and arm sometimes, and I'm like, 'Excuse me?' But I'm getting that wrong. Hold on. Let me tell you why I don't think you should avoid looking at me. It's not that I'm your father. I mean, I want you to love me and treat me the same as everyone else. That's what all this is about. You don't look away from somebody because you've been taught not to stare. If you want to look, you can look. That's just the way it is. But don't treat people like they're invisible," I say. "Even though they want to be sometimes, you know?"

"You want to be invisible?"

"It's complicated," I say. "I just want you to think I'm interesting."

"I think you're interesting."

"What for?"

"Because you're deformed and you scare all my friends." She's joking, has this look on her face. She tells me about all the scary things I've ever done. She tells me when her friend Laney had slipped into the ditch and banged her knee on cement and I'd picked her up and carried her to the house, Laney hadn't been thinking of her knee but of my wrist, touching her, of my ear, so close to Laney's cheek. Joy says she's explained what a preemie is and that my ear isn't the result of a malformation but the lack of formation. She says sometimes she dreams of getting my ear in her mouth. She remembers being the counselor at a school for boys, in one life, and a boy coming in with his head wrapped in bandages, a bicycle mishap, and all the other boys thinking there was something wrong with him, how they pointed fingers, and she'd had to help him with lessons between his classes because he was just so sad and he couldn't face the world alone anymore or something. She couldn't help thinking how funny the boy looked. "The whole act of looking at people," she said to me in her grown-up voice. "That's natural, just like you said, isn't it?"

Later in the evening I ask the question that's been on my mind, lately. "Does Laurie hate me? Do you even know? Does she even listen to me? Does she even care?"

Joy is holding the cat. Her hair is done up and feathered, with a green ribbon. "She hates you sometimes. Other times she likes you fine," she says.

"Does Bill hate me?"

"Bill doesn't really know you. 'Hate' is a strong word."

I don't know where my daughter learned to talk this way. *Hate is* rather than *hate's*, the way she elongates, lowers her eyelids, purses her lips at the sound of *word*. It's not like having a conversation with a nine-year-old. I think maybe she's heard the words from somebody else. Or maybe she's retained the information from some other life. The more I hear her speak, the more I learn to appreciate the sound of her voice.

Once there was a yak. There was also a man with a small arm who would whip the yak until the yak did as the man asked. I hauled baskets of rice, blankets, wild animals, women, children, and the man with the small arm. We walked on a road overlooking a mountain. The sky was always gray, the grass always dark. I lived with a herd sometimes. Sometimes I was surrounded by people. I had a sore on my back, and life was cold. But when you live as a yak, you don't even feel the cold. You feel your owner beating you with his whip. You feel the weight of small children when they climb onto your neck. In Mongolia, there were ditches full of icy water that the man broke open with the butt of his stick. In Mongolia, there were good days and bad days, days when you didn't eat your grain and the man was so reminded of his father, who, in his last moments, wouldn't touch any food; the man was so reminded of his children, who kept getting sick, and they had no medicine. There were days when the snow would come down like feathers and when rain fell in ribbons, days when the air turned so dry and cold that my nose bled. There were days when I'd go out behind the stable for peace, to feel the wind, to tilt my head down and consider whatever it is yaks consider, become unused. There were days I'd go out behind the stable for solitude, and the man would already be there, staring at nothing.

SKIN

My fingers were outgrowing my skin. On the ReDox machine, the red light that normally blinked wasn't blinking, and my biological fingertips (made up of 97% plasmodium-based gelatinous tissue, which could harden if not treated) were starting to break through the dry, synthetic fingertips. So I would have to both figure out how to stop growing and get my ReDox machine working, which would probably require a lot of time and money. A new slab of skin would make my insurance soar through the roof.

I thought of all the protists who didn't have synthetic skin. I knew how to be a better human—I stayed clean, I went to work, and I went home, I socialized. Bryce and I adopted an old dog for a while, and eventually it died, and we were sad. We had two friends: Ellis and Deidra, a couple, like us, except they were human. Bryce grew plants on the balcony and took photographs of insects on the leaves. I built model trains. We talked about adopting a child, a protist like us, but neither of us felt we could afford a child at the moment.

When I finally felt okay enough about my hands to show Bryce, she seemed perturbed. Shocked. I had begun to let myself go, she must have thought. She had experienced similar bodily outbursts when we started dating—the dimple on her stomach where her skin had been enclosed around her had burst and released a miasma of spores— but she had at least gotten it taken care of quickly before she spread throughout the dorm hall.

"Are you ashamed of me?"

She held my hand next to the bathroom sink and studied the exposure of my real tissue, the gnarled purple reeds beginning to poke their way through.

"It's all about the lotion," she said. "I'm not ashamed of you." There was a hesitant quiver to her voice. Like she wanted to give me advice but couldn't find the human words to get it out.

The more I tried to convince myself that I was human, the less human I felt.

"Just give me some time. I'm going to help you get this worked out," she said.

"I either need to fix my skin or stop growing," I said.

Bryce did at least give me a kiss before heading out, but it wasn't enough to keep me satiated. I couldn't tell if her eyes had been open or shut. I hoped she had shut her eyes. I wanted things to go on as usual between us.

Bryce went out of town to see her parents. I called the ReDox manufacturer and asked who I could get for repairs. They sent a tiny old man with this big leather tool bag. He dropped down beside the ReDox machine and twisted one of the knobs off of the big black square on the bottom.

"This is where the problems usually start," he said.

He twirled a pipe cleaner around in the box. He looked up at me and back down at his work. Probably when he was young, there were no such things as protists. He was probably not even awake to the world when our spores burst from the underworld and assimilated and restructured.

"I'm going to give you some space," I said.

The synthetic skin had totally unraveled from around my hands. My shoulders were starting to bulge. He looked at me with those eyes, like he had never seen anything like me before. Give me just a minute to assimilate,

I wanted to tell him. I didn't know why I had such terrifying, crazy thoughts. "Assimilation" was not a word I liked to think about.

I was starting to feel like the protist-alpha living off of the highway, who lived in culverts and at the entrances of sewers and grew a hallucinogenic drug on their backs, which they ate off one another. When they came out from the culverts, you absolutely, positively knew they weren't human—they were protists, long armed and mesodermic, their curvatures hardened, no way they'd ever fit in any synthetic skin.

I grew up horrified at the thought of homelessness and potentially losing my humanity. My adoptive parents were two humans from Texas. Shortly after finishing junior college, I sold and rented washers, driers, and refrigerators. My girlfriend, Bryce, had gone to a four-year college and wrote instruction manuals for the company that manufactures ReDox machines. When I came to the city, she was living in a town house and had a car, an ex-husband (human) about four blocks away. Now she had every reason to abandon me to whatever it is I was going through.

I was afraid of leaving the house looking like the kind of person normal people would not want to associate with. I would be an easy target for the police. Protists who lost their sense of humanity tended to let themselves go back to their roots, and sometimes protist-alphas became wall huggers, flattened and stretched over the bodies of abandoned cars and playground equipment. They became formless and melted into one another, released spores and burst and spread and, eventually, became mindless as black mold. And then everyone, humans and protists alike, would have to come in and clean up the mess.

Inside me, I knew what my body was capable of stretching itself to, and what frightened me was I didn't know how to keep this thing from growing, extending its arms beyond my arms, infesting everything around me. I had read a magazine theorizing a roaming protist who would infest and cover entire buildings, becoming unrecognizable, a mega structure with eyes so big they wouldn't even look like eyes, eyes in holes and in walls and in furnishings, until everything would become unrecognizable, the protist big and wide as a mountain.

Bryce laid me down on the table and asked to look at my back. She traced her fingers along the edges of my spine down to my tailbone, where she gave me a good squeeze.

"The muscles are taut," she said. "Yours. No. You have a bubble right here. Like, right here along these ridges. Feel that?"

She tried to pop the bubble with her fingertips.

"I don't feel anything."

"It looks like a sack of quarters in there."

Bryce made us coffee. She had hands like a warrior and wore rings on every finger, even on her thumbs. She told me that I shouldn't put much hope in the prospect of my skin recovering from the dehydration, that I could always just get a new slab, could come by skin pretty cheap, that my real problem was with the growing. I'd already started cracking in other areas besides my fingers, especially around my elbows and the backs of my knees. The sun blared down and burned my scalp. I started to lose feeling in my forehead. I felt hot and disconnected. I suddenly realized there was no point in being interested in things: eating, having a relationship, fitting in with humans, looking at pictures of animals. This was called being depressed. And this was why so many protists let themselves go. When I finished eating, I soaked in water for nearly an hour, trying to shake the feeling of worthlessness. Particles of blue mold seeped out of my cracked chest. I listened to the radio in the other room. When I got out of the tub, I ate again. Yeah, I think "depression" was a word that fit the bill: I was faced with a sort of human mortality that wouldn't result in my death but the eradication of consciousness (studies have shown that even black mold is capable of instinctively expressing pain but has no consciousness). I looked down and realized I'd eaten an entire tub of ice cream. I wondered if all the eating was somehow related to potential antisocial tendencies.

Except I knew antisocial behavior when I saw it. I wore bandages on my elbows and hands. On the way home from work, a protist-alpha stepped onto the bus and looked with its mold-encrusted formlessness toward me, as if acknowledging it had once been like me. I ignored him/her and pretended there was something outside the window.

But he/she smelled me, came to me and asked in the deep, unfiltered voice of a woman if I had a cigarette. A dark receptacle opened at the top of her head, presumably where she wanted me to place the cigarette.

"Sorry, I don't have anything."

A sliver of brown arm hung off what appeared to be a red knuckle. People were moving away from her, holding their noses. A brown mist wafted from a hard lump grown on her shoulder-sloped membrane.

She found a seat near the doors and made a ball of herself. Then she opened up like a volcano, revealing jointed tentacles and a purple endoplasmic material that, when the tentacles began to quiver, flung onto the windows and seats and ceiling.

Everyone cleared off the bus. Then I was alone, and I was thinking about myself and whether I would want to be left alone on a bus at night with no one to help— the bus driver even too scared to stay on board—when things cleared up for me, what would I do, what would I feel?

"Are you okay?"

She said in a voice echoing a sort of quasi-forgotten humanity, "I AM FORGETTING MY MOTHER'S NAME."

I called the police. When the operator asked what the emergency was, I didn't know how to say that there was a protist on the bus that was going through a deep psychological regression. She was forgetting her assigned lineage—whatever human had taken her in as a young protist pancake, raised her, given her experiences, all of it was being forgotten. Sometimes it happened with a trigger. Probably too much bullying at work. Probably someone had commented on the way her eyes bulged from her skull, the way her ears hung, the way her skin flaked and splotched. Some protists just had better-quality synthetic skin than others.

"CAN YOU HELP ME."

"I called the police," I said. "They can help you."

A scorpion's tail came out of the head and flopped to the floor. I knew the looks of this. Some kind of anger, some kind of break-boned, fuck-all attitude swirl. She was angry I'd called the police. She was in some sort of philosophical agony that it had finally come to this.

"Are you okay?"

"I AM FORGETTING MY MOTHER'S NAME."

"Don't you want to smoke a cigarette?"

I pulled a pack of cigarettes out of my bag and held them out to her.

I didn't want to talk about anyone's mother.

She swung her scorpion's tail and struck me on the shoulder. I could feel my inner tissue bulge where the tail had pierced my skin.

Outside, there was a parking lot and the shopping mall and a line of trees hiding what looked to be a 24/7 clinic. I stayed on the bus because that's what I would have wanted someone to do for me.

I sat with her until the police came, one protist and one human. No questions asked, the protist cop injected her with muscle relaxants and molded her into the shape of the big, purple, oval box the human cop carried with her. Then the protist cop splatted the woman into the case and shut the lid.

"I'm fine," I said.

The protist cop wrote something down, looking at the walls of the car.

The case jostled around, and the regular cop propped her knee onto it.

He looked at my hands. The bandages had come off. "Is that because of this?"

"No, I've not been well."

They left, and I stayed there with the spores and guts of the woman that'd exploded all over the place. The driver came back wearing a mask and told me that I had to get off the bus, that he had to explain to his boss what happened, that they were going to have to get an ammonia crew to scrub the bus before any spores spread, but they wouldn't get everything, not every little bit of cellular matter left behind by the sputtering woman.

The bus driver seemed to think it was my fault. He looked at my hands and gagged.

"They're not that bad," Ellis said, looking at my hands. But he and his fiancé, Deidra, wouldn't touch me. At least they were very honest about why: "It's not that we think we're going to catch anything," Ellis said. "It's just kind of gross. I mean, look at it."

"I wouldn't touch you either if you were open," I said.

"See what I mean?"

I raised my purple appendages at Deidra's face. Sick looking, she fled to the bathroom. "You want to touch it?" I waved my hands in front of Ellis.

"Get that out of here," he said. "Can you make them smaller?"

I explained very briefly that this was a growth spurt probably caused by depression or some psychosocial issue, and while I could fit my hands into a bowl and eventually they would take on the shape of the bowl, I could not make my hands any smaller. In fact, if exposed to the air for much longer, they risked a permanent hardening, which, as it turns out, was reversible but would require surgical removal of the hardened tissue.

"Well, okay," Ellis said.

We were having a sort of game night. To help ease my mind. And to ironically celebrate my surviving the incident on the bus. Bryce was in the other room, looking for the Monopoly board. She could be heard humming to herself. Then a muffled sort of howl.

"Deidra is thinking about leaving me," Ellis said.

"What for?"

Ellis shook his head. It took him a moment to say that neither of them was ready to get married, but he'd been the only one trying at their relationship: Deidra had become more of an apparition in their house than a person.

"So you agree with her?"

"I don't know," he said.

I didn't find either Ellis or Deidra attractive. Although human, neither of the two had insides that melded with the exterior. Both could be described with a few of the same characteristics: they had large folds under their arms, and they washed only occasionally. They wore button-ups and denim shorts. Ellis had a stud in one ear, and Deidra had a blue streak on the side of her head. I thought sometimes of the differences in our being: while humans are made up of many different components, my insides consist mostly of one material. I'd been compared to a single-celled organism (more like algae than bacteria, though we thrive in the bacteria-rich underground). I could reach into myself and not be hurt: the belly button, the entry point into my synthetic skin, was also a playground for my unicellular hand. The cloud of my tissue was comforting.

Then I heard Bryce's howl again. I went and found her leaning into the closet. Mold bubbled up the side of the wall, and near the middle of the hairy strand imbedded in the plaster was the rogue eye, brown and hungry like mine.

"Foster," she said.

I came and saw the eye. It looked up at me in confusion.

"We have to kill it," she said.

"We have to," I said. Absolutely, positively, I wasn't thinking of anything but the eye and how to kill it and how whatever this was could not possibly be from anyone but me—I had spread to the house somehow.

I went to the kitchen, where Ellis was standing drinking a beer, looking into the living room at Deidra, who wanted to leave him.

"I'm sorry about dumping this on you," Ellis said.

"Yeah?"

"I know what you're thinking."

I grabbed the spatula.

"No, it's fine. Excuse me," I said.

Bryce and I tried to get the eye out with the spatula. I shoved the corner into the plaster, which had softened around the eye, and pried the thing out. Then we dropped it in a plastic bag and threw the bag in the garbage.

"Let me see your fingers."

"Just go."

"You need to be careful. You're making spores. Right here."

I realized how much Bryce meant to me. She didn't care about the way I looked. She was miserable, and she wanted to take care of me, and I didn't know how much longer she would be able to hold out.

I asked, "So what happens to you if you cover the side of a mountain? Is that like an extension of you? What's that all about?"

Bryce's father had not been able to blow his nose properly. He blew his nose with only one hand and always got his DNA on the wall over the toilet. The headboard smelled of her grandmother's hair for months after she died. She grew up with some idea of what contamination was all about. And so she was starting to feel scared for me. I was leaking an aromatic liquid out of cracks in my skin. I started sitting in the tub. I read books. I didn't want to infect the rest of the apartment. But Bryce was trying to keep me calm.

"There's a fruit fly in the bathroom I can't get rid of," she said.

"It's not hurting anything," I said.

Bryce spit into the sink. She had a date with Deidra in an hour. I felt bad for her: she was walking out of one mess and into another. I wanted to talk to her about the growth in me and the growth we were capable of and how to get rid of this thing growing inside of me and what it meant to grow from the seed of a tree in the ground into a towering monstrosity of carbon—

what was it like to be human? I wanted to ask. There could be no better feeling than being constricted to one's biological skin.

Also: I wanted to talk about my body, but the shape of my body was unknown to me. There were facets to a body I was unfamiliar with. The image of a cell on a poster might be shaped like a planet, an inverted, budding organism beneath a layer of deteriorating skin. I could talk about what I didn't know about my body. I didn't know whether I had one or two center points, what those centers contained, whether they were like the nuclei of a cell or something much more complicated. I'd seen illustrations of protists floating in spherical orbs, those orbs floating in larger bodies of translucent tissue. I didn't know where my brain was located. I didn't know whether I was as protected from the elements as people say.

I'd also seen alphas hanging from slivers of flesh under bridges, unhappy knots in the complicated shapes of cellular confusion. They were scooped off the cement and placed into boxes and, presumably, taken to government labs where they were thrown into vats of algae.

The repairman delivered the ReDox machine back into the apartment. It had a new component on the end, which he said was a cheapish cooling unit that I would need to replace once every six months or else learn how to refill myself. He showed me the red light at the top, which blinked momentarily before shutting down again. He wrote something down on his tablet, and I signed it with a cold knuckle, and he went out the door as quickly as he'd come in.

The machine inside was cold and sterile. There was an oily smudge on the white bar close to where my face went.

The machine filled with a pink gel. I breathed through a tube. My skin swelled with moisture and the pink gel's nutrients.

Then I had to get skin grafts. All the damage from my growing had really taken a toll on the skin.

"It was just your body trying to get away from you," the doctor said. "Your ReDox was broken for how long?"

"A month or so."

"That makes sense. You'll stop growing now. My theory is your body detected it could break through the skin and get free." He pressed along my back with gloved fingers. "There's some hardening along here." He tapped with a pen. "Rub some hot rocks on it, and that should loosen you up."

Part of me had already been scraped off the wall, thrown into a plastic bag, tossed into the bin, taken by a truck to wherever it is they take garbage. I closed my eyes and tried to see where I'd gone. I saw a blurred landscape that wasn't a landscape. I saw a tree on a hill. Birds flitted through pieces of metal. And I was spreading, not thin, but really growing, covering the landscape, becoming something more than just the imitation of a human. But then I was back at home and thinking to myself that it couldn't have been real, that the eye was in a plastic bag. Everything else was in my head.

I wanted to leave Bryce. I told her over dinner. "I've been thinking about being single," I said. Because there was something I wanted to find, and I had the whim that I didn't feel the same for Bryce anymore. "I'm sorry I didn't tell you sooner. I wanted to, but."

"I don't think that's going to work," she said. "Who'll take care of you?"

"I'll take care of myself."

"You know I'm the one that should be dumping you," she said, biting her knuckle. "I just don't understand how anyone could let themselves go like that."

I didn't argue with her. I knew exactly what she was feeling. I was relieved, honestly. She loved me, must have loved me, since she stayed with me through my ordeal, but there was just something about me she hadn't been able to handle, exactly. A thick, purple substance oozed down her hand from her knuckles.

"So are you kicking me out or not?"

"No. I don't think that's a good idea." Kicking Bryce out was a very human thing to do, but I figured I could find the mega structure with or without her. And she was right: there was no one else who would take care of me in my condition.

"Do you even love me?"

"I do love you," I said.

"Then why do you want to leave me?" She wiped her hand clean on the tablecloth and went into the bathroom and brushed her teeth.

That night, we slept closer than we had in a while. I wrapped my hands around her. I could feel my way inside her: through the bellybutton, her phosphorescent insides, imitation human flesh closing against my hand, trying to conceal what was inside her. Her body was a beautiful body. What was inside Bryce was the same thing that was inside me.

My hands began to recede little by little, and soon I would be able to sew my synthetic fingers shut. Things would return to normal. Furthermore, I felt a renewed human energy in me, beginning with my feelings for Bryce: she was the one for me, as humans say. Despite this, I thought constantly about life after death. Not the same as I had before, when I had been filled with a sort of cosmic dread. Because now I felt there was a chance I could be reborn into something greater, after my inevitable demise.

On the other hand, the playful cynic in me said there was no such thing as anything greater than my current state of being. There were people who looked different, or bigger or smaller, but life after the death of the body felt like an impossibility. I was born the size of a pancake, was raised in a cage, grew in a human household, and eventually stopped growing, like all protists who would come to imitate humanity. Because the only way I could survive was to inherit human physicality and personality traits and therefore their sympathy, I never grew beyond human potential. Which also meant, I thought, that I could never be anything greater than my current state of being. And one day my synthetic skin would rot away, leaving the husk of mold, which would harden to a crust. If I continued being human.

I was scientific about it, about as scientific as a naïve explorer of the urban underground could be. For the mega structure to exist, it would have to make the conscious choice to spread itself physically into something beyond human capability. This would require the possibility of moving beyond human emotion in order to disregard the fear of becoming one with the landscape. Practically, such a being could not have friends, could not have dogs, cats, a place to live except the environment itself. They could not have money, nor a job, they would not have the problems other people have, and they would not feel the same happiness. The happiness of the mega structure would be an alien concept to everyone else. The very air I breathed, if I would breathe at all, could be a sort of happiness. This in itself felt like a kind of enlightenment.

I looked everywhere. In the city there were many opportunities for dispersal and contamination: those were the human words for it, anyway. Sentient mold, disregarded parts, eyeballs poking out of cracks. Bryce stayed supportive of me. But she wouldn't come. "Tell me what you find," she said, indifferent to the whole idea. As long as I was having fun and didn't get caught trespassing.

Alone, armed only with a flashlight and my cell phone's camera, I dropped down into a grate and searched around the darkest portions of the city. Every night, I found a way into a new hole, a new sewer, closed-off subway tunnels. Alphas lived under there in the dark, hundreds of them. They dragged shopping carts and mattresses and tables and chairs into brick aqueducts and set up shop, even among stalagmites of the dry dead. The living would stay quietly and sadly until a new skyscraper went up and zoning restrictions happened and all of them were forced out, rehoused, and forced out again. I stopped shining light in their eyes. I stopped asking questions. They didn't know what I meant by a big, omnipresent ancestor of the protist. The idea was stupid. They seemed less interested in me than the food I offered—the human stuff, fried chicken and canned beans and heads of dissolving lettuce in plastic bags.

I squeezed through a hole and came out into a brick and concrete tunnel. A human woman lived in the tunnel with her cats. Her home looked like an altar. She told me there were eyes watching her—the city had placed eyes all along the walls, in dirty splotches that reeked of mold. I thought she was talking about motion detectors or cameras, but I took it as an opportunity, a good sign, that something living was watching her not with ill intent but happy curiosity. To Bryce's dismay, I started crawling deeper.

So deep I could no longer feel the rumble of the subway. And despite the absence of humanity, the scarcity of light, I didn't feel alone. I, too, started to feel watched. But I couldn't find anything. I came down into the tunnels for over a month, but I couldn't find any eyes, noses, mold of any kind. Only once did I nearly get caught by workers, who I assumed were looking over the foundation of an old railway. Their lights bobbed toward me through the garbage heaps and stagnant puddles. I hid in a tunnel stairwell and went home after they had cleared out.

On the last day I went exploring, I found a trail of purple mold leading to a metal switch box. I shined a light up around the brickwork and saw a dozen or so rods of purple cartilage stretching out of pipes to the floor, where roots twisted from pillows of mold and wrapped around the switch box and slithered in through the cracks. A claw grew out of the side of the box. An eyeball looked from one of the claw's bulbous knuckles past a thick film of pink flesh. And that's when I changed my mind about immortality and enlightenment. My human chest heaved involuntary, simulated human breaths of despair. The eye rolled slightly and looked at me. I thought: I want to touch this thing so I can say I've come close to immortality. It was a stupid thought, but

I've heard humans say the same about being at a funeral when they were kids, being hung by the arms of parents over cold, dead relatives, the feeling of being close to something you can't figure out, not yet anyway. I reached out and touched the claw. When I let go of the claw it flinched, extended toward me, and drooped back down again. My chest kept heaving. Everything became still.

ANIMAL EXPERT

In the summer of 1997, I worked as an animal expert
in Brooklyn, Michigan, and for a while my best friend
was a baby kangaroo. I kept him in a sack and let him
live with me in my rental. He followed me around
everywhere. He always wanted to be in the same place
as me, and so when he aged out and I finally had to let
him go, my heart was broken. My animal entertainment
agency got me another young kangaroo to raise and
grow attached to. They kept me in animal supply, which
was enough to keep me going. It's safe to say I was doing
it for the kangaroos.

The agency paid the rent on my trailer and gave me
a credit card to spend on animal products, fence repairs,
shipping containers, etc. I became a kangaroo expert
quickly and just fairly okay at everything else. If you can
count to three, you can learn to be an animal expert.
Kangaroos wore diapers and acted like any regular pet.
They could be dangerous, but that goes for just about
any animal. My father, for instance, tripped over the dog
one night and fell down the steps. My sister's cockatoo,
when she was little, tried to chew her eyelids open
when it got out of the cage one night. But I got so badly
attached to Mr. Moss, an Eastern grey kangaroo, I told

my agency roughly near the date they'd have to take him back that he'd bounced into the road and gotten hit by a car. I'd been throwing him a kind of going-away party when he'd gotten killed. I even made up a story about how he'd bounced at just the right angle and gotten lodged in the windshield, and the driver, whoever it was, had driven off in a hurry with Mr. Moss still embedded in the glass.

Mr. Moss secretly continued living with me in my tiny home. He slept at the foot of the bed at night, and nobody bothered us. "Please, no more kangaroos," I said. I told them I couldn't handle the emotional turmoil anymore and I needed to move on to something else. This worked because the animal market fluctuated so rapidly—children didn't care how sweet or fascinating diaper-wearing kangaroos could be—their brains were connected to the television and media and whatever animal popped up in the newest cartoons. When I was their age, though, I had dreams of working with all types of animals, of expressing myself through them. But I learned early in my career that it's very hard to find meaning when consumer markets shift like leaves, when we live in an ecosystem of child-brained idiots.

Being surrounded by so many children, I was constantly reminded of myself as a kid, how I never knew what to do with myself. I feel that I know less now than I did back then. I've always had nightmares about the time when my father took me to look at ostriches at a farm. At the time I was impressed by their big, powerful legs, the way they bent and stretched when they moved slowly around the enclosure. We came home with two big, shimmering eggs. When I was alone, I wanted to hold them. But it grew cold in the house, and as I held both of the shells, something pushed me, and I dropped both eggs, and they shattered on the kitchen floor. I never knew how to explain what had pushed me, how I had dropped the eggs. My father looked at the broken eggs and said, "You were holding them both at once?" After that, he never forgot how stupid I had been: a mother ostrich had worked hard to make those eggs, and I had broken them. What were we doing with them to begin with, then? I wanted to ask him. We had perfectly good chicken eggs. What was the point?

I barely knew how to do anything else my agency asked me to do, but I always said yes to a job. Komodo dragons were really just big, aggressive dogs that you could put on a leash and drag around like luggage. Foxes were hyper: I loved them, but they made everything smell bad. I tried keeping them in the house for a while, but they burrowed holes into the couch and left urine everywhere. I always said no to ostriches, though. They mortified me with their big, dinosaur feet and their long, sturdy necks: I saw them often at zoos but never went near their fences. After the lie about the kangaroo, though, things got weird. For instance, there was a box with a toad as big as my head in it. My job was to get the toad in and out of the box without allowing its skin to come into contact with human skin, and to keep it moisturized for the duration of the show. The kids loved it.

They also put me in a show with rats. They really aren't my favorite animal, so I found a method that minimized my contact time with them. I took the box with the rat in it and asked two children to hold a board. They held on to the board while I said rat-related facts, then dumped the rat on one of their heads. The rat climbed down their shoulder and got on the board and crawled to the other child holding up the other side of the board, where it then climbed onto their head and ate the treat I'd placed there. Usually the room was so invigorated by this that they didn't even notice how afraid of rats I was.

The last time I worked exclusively in front of children was at a school in Carson, Mississippi. I had a few elementary teachers come down to assist me with a big Amazonian python. They held it out at length for me to show off its size. Then it started to wrap around me. It got onto my head like a scarf and choked the breath out of me, and I fell flat on my back, snake and all, nobody helping. It must have looked like part of the show to them.

There's a video out there somewhere of all those hundreds of kids laughing at me, not knowing anything about death or suffocation, and I wonder whether any of them for that matter would have been affected by my death had it actually happened, whether their parents would have talked to them about the sadness of death and loneliness and how they should think about where I was now, this person they didn't know whose eyeballs had popped out of his head, and where I'd been all my life up until that moment, and where I had been going.

Somehow I did not die, and a few television producers who saw the video were impressed that I had successfully demonstrated the python's strength on camera, and because it was an accident, my agent considered it ethically exploitable. But as I lay on the couch at home— my jaw wired shut for two weeks, neck and head bruised from being crunched by the snake—I had a lot of time to think about the direction my life was headed in. I thought a lot about the way I interacted with people outside of my job. If someone recognized me as the animal guy, I nodded my head and said things like, "You look familiar too. Who are you again? I love your jacket. Where did you get that?" During events, I was capable of speaking with eloquence, of keeping children's attention, waving my arms to a hypnotic rhythm that kept them sated, glued to their auditorium floor. The only thing I was required to do was talk about the snake or rat or kangaroo or bundle of fur with eyes on it and engage with the audience in some way. I'd boom out like a lunatic, "Who wants to put this rat on their head?" But outside of work I was useless. My relationships with my parents, sister, ex-girlfriends all petered into nothing worth talking about. I talked to Mr. Moss about this in half sentences. This was the way I'd done things up to this point—I knew he didn't understand me, but I needed to talk anyway, so my words came out in shorthand, a murmur. He looked around nervously at the house. I didn't take his movements as any sort of response.

When my jaw was unwired and I returned to my job, I got on pretty well with one of the show's stagehands, a single mother, Miranda, who also loved animals. Her daughter, Jill, loved the shit out of ostriches. They both grew up near an ostrich farm, and Miranda kept all the pictures of ostriches Jill drew in a binder. "Have I got a thing for you," I said. So I brought them home to meet Mr. Moss, who was up to my chest by then, still wearing diapers, and angry as hell at everything. This was supposed to be a date, too—"You want to come meet my kangaroo?" I'd asked Miranda in private. By this time we'd been out a few times, pecked one another on the lips, so I felt comfortable inviting her and her kid to my house.

When they arrived, Mr. Moss stood there against the closet with his arms crooked under his breasts, looking sidelong at us as we entered. He poofed his chest out. "Who's this?" I said in the singsong voice of animal-speak, trying to keep him calm. I told Miranda that she should go in and try to talk with him, that he wouldn't hurt her, and Miranda said, "Well, I'll have a roll around the floor with him," and immediately Mr. Moss put her in a headlock and started kicking her shins. Jill screamed. I couldn't move. Miranda pulled the comforter off the bed and broke my bedside lamp trying to get away from him and managed to pull herself up off the floor. Bloodied, bruised, one of her fingers bent back in a ninety-degree angle, Miranda grabbed her screaming daughter and limped out immediately. Mr. Moss retreated back to his corner and got down low, probably knowing he'd really messed this up for me.

Miranda had to wear a cast for a month, and people started asking questions about what had left kangaroo marks on her skin.

My agent suspected that I'd lied about Mr. Moss getting hit by the car. Plus, Miranda had blatantly stated that it was a kangaroo-related injury, despite promising she'd keep it to herself. She wasn't about to lie for somebody she'd just met, and I guess I don't blame her for that.

I hid Mr. Moss in the shed out back, which doubled as an extra bedroom. I put a padlock on the door and claimed the landlord was saving the place for someone else. Shutting him in there was one of the hardest things I'd ever done. All night I could hear him scratching, things falling over.

There was a bit of in-house shuffling around as a result of the leftover publicity from the python incident. By some marketing miracle, I was invited to go onto Leno in the event another guest cancelled. The thing about the snake had taken off in the news, and I was seen as nationally daring and interesting. I really hoped I didn't have to be funny: I wasn't funny at all, unless I was being strangled by a snake, which I guess is sort of funny if you're the right kind of person.

I had a Komodo on a leash. I walked her all over the front of the stage, and Leno stood back, microphone against his lips like he wanted to say something. When she hissed at the audience, everyone swooned. Then I brought out a bird that was bigger than most children. The cassowary strutted around on the stage irrespective of me and gave everyone the look. It made a lunge at Leno, and he ran circles around his desk, laughing, but if the thing jumped Leno, there was nothing I could do to stop the carnage. I knew I wouldn't be coming back again. In the parking lot, the bird jumped on my back, and three of my people had to get her off. Leno showed a clip of the cassowary in the next episode's monologue. He made jokes about how I was the worst animal handler he'd ever seen. Big laughs. He even made a jab about how I'd been tackled in the parking lot.

Sometimes when I was feeling down, I'd go out to the shed and coax Mr. Moss into holding me. There was something there, between the two of us; I didn't want to be in the presence of humans any more than I wanted to look at myself in the mirror. When I looked at myself in the mirror, brushing my teeth, I saw my face as it'd been on the television.

My agent got me a public access show, good for a few episodes. A variety of animals ran around on the table: birds, rabbits, a dog, turtles. I loved that we put in regular household pets next to what children might consider to be exotic, the better to explore the uniqueness of each individual animal—particularly because a child, with no remorse, might pick up a turtle and hide it in her closet for however long before it died. But then the turtle latched onto the dog's nose in one episode, and you think that sort of thing would be comedy gold, but a lot of parents were upset about the way the dog had screamed, the devilish look in the turtle's eyes, the bit of blood, and how I just stood there—it wasn't supposed to be that real, viewer letters suggested.

But you know, these are animals, I said. They can't be trained not to bite each other. I mean, how does one train a turtle not to bite? I was happy at least no one laughed about the dog being bitten. We deserved all the letters we'd gotten for that.

My producer didn't let me respond to the letters. They had Miranda working in the back, responding to all sorts of fan mail. I'd suggested her for the part since we knew each other somewhat intimately. There was a stack of letters from children, all of them asking about animals. Mostly school projects. One kid asked whether I had a favorite animal, and Miranda responded (I had to read this aloud on television) that I loved manatees. I'd never seen a manatee in my life. There was one letter from a kid asking if I'd ever hurt or forgotten to feed an animal before, since that's what'd happened to his bearded dragon, and I actually drafted a response: *The only animal that deserves to be hurt is you, Matthew. You ungrateful little shit. You believe your parents bought you a bearded dragon because they wanted you to learn responsibility? Not hardly. They wanted to shut you up. Everything they do for you is to keep you from ruining what's still left to ruin.* I was upset that the boy had lost the bearded dragon, not native to Wisconsin, definitely not native to that evil little shit's house. Miranda's response was the one I had to read on the air: *Sometimes we lose things, and animals want to be free.* At least she was right.

We tried to make things work though Miranda said no kangaroos. Her daughter was still traumatized. "I like those kinds of animals on set, but that's it," she said. I told her I doubted they would renew me for any more episodes, anyway, since I kept getting too many things wrong. The animals were always biting and clawing at each other, and I wasn't trained to make animals get along. What I wanted to do was pick up turtles off the side of the road for a living. My father used to find gopher turtles near his home and shoot them and bury them in the backyard because he didn't want the government to come and make us move. I used to lay in bed at night and mutter to myself incoherently beneath the sheets. Turtles were slow, and they didn't do anything. Kids used to pick them up and paint their shells. I wanted to help all animals—get them unstuck from the corners humans put them into. I wouldn't even mind going under someone's house if an animal got stuck there. But I'd been told that kind of job came with a pretty hard caveat: a lot of the animals I removed would be dead or dying, and I'd have to deal with that probably more often than living animals. But that was okay, I thought. I could do good by them.

In any case, Miranda had forgiven me for everything that happened, and she was willing to give me another shot, so long as I could go about things normally.

"Where's the kangaroo?" she asked.

"Sold him," I said.

Miranda had a lot of cats, all different looking, living inside the house with her and Jill. Six or seven cats, but aside from window blinds with holes in them, their house was clean. I have a theory about cats: that they aren't like dogs at all. Dogs can understand what you're saying most of the time, like Mr. Moss, and—more importantly—cats don't have a sense of humor, but they have plenty of natural curiosity and a lot of aggression that reminds me of human aggression, which is to say that I believe people love cats so much because they are like a natural extension of the human psyche, an emotion in physical form that can't be expressed by humans under normal social circumstances. We see cats as being like bits of ourselves rather than companions. They wander off into the night and get into fights, have litters of kittens, cry even when they've been well taken care of. When I was growing up, I once saw my father pick up a cat by the tail, swing it around in an arc, and toss it over the fence because it had scratched my back when a firecracker went off. Miranda's thing with cats was good. And as a result, I tried to be understanding when she said that she could not maintain a normal relationship. Two or three days a week, even, was too much for her.

What was odd about Miranda and these cats, though, is she didn't seem to care what they did to Jill. The little girl would be sitting there trying to pet one, and the cat would whop Jill on the head with claws extended, just whopping the hell out of her for no reason. This kept happening: Jill would sit there, and the cat wouldn't stop hitting her, and Miranda thought this was just wonderful. And I'd seen Miranda pinch Jill's legs for any small infraction—walking too slow behind her, knocking into a stack of empty boxes when she was there with us at the office, excited to see some animals. Of course, the thing with the cat could be funny, but what if one of them hit Jill's eye? What if the cat took her eye out? "They're harmless," Miranda said to me, watching her daughter getting her face beaten by the cat, red whelps swelling up and bleeding. Jill didn't even try to move away. That's when I noticed how the little girl looked unhappy most of the time.

One night, not long after getting back together with Miranda, I had a dream that I was hired by a movie producer to go into his whale's mouth to remove the lumpy calcium deposits, big as soccer balls. I woke up in a sweat. Miranda wasn't there. I went out to the shed and hung out with Mr. Moss for a couple hours before he started to get restless. I tried to tell him about my dream, but like most humans, other people's dreams were uninteresting to him. He kept going to a crack in the shed where he'd been clawing. He looked out through the hole. He put his hands up to the wall and got his eye as close to the crack and the outside as possible. This is the part where I say that I knew what I had to do: I was with Miranda now, and she'd leave me if I didn't get rid of Mr. Moss. She'd maybe even call the police or tell my agent, which was worse. I didn't want to go to jail or lose my job. I pushed back against the idea of getting rid of him. I gave him some hay and scratched him behind the ear. Then he turned on me, hay in his mouth like a rat's nest and eyes bulging. I came out of the shed with what would become a scar above my right eye and a broken nose. I cried myself to sleep. Later, when I went out to check on him again, he'd curled himself into the wall, unable to look at me. I tried touching his kangaroo shoulder: sloped, though muscular, patches of fur rough from having pressed against the wood.

When I was asked to do a presentation on ostrich eggs, I said no. But Miranda persisted. She knew I had all these nightmares about ostriches, getting pecked and stomped to death by them, but she assured me that people rode them all the time all over the world in races. What did I have to worry about? It could be therapeutic. Face my fears and all. A lot could be fixed about me if I just did something with ostriches. So I said okay, I'd do a presentation on the eggs: I'd hold two at once, and nothing would push me and make me drop them. But Miranda said I needed to include the mother somehow, too, do something with motherhood. In what way does the mother protect its young from harm? She was personally interested, but I was not because I didn't want to get hurt again. The scar on my face from Mr. Moss was still fresh, and I might have been having trouble seeing out of my right eye.

But this could have been from sleeping so hard on that side of my face. I thought my head was full of fluid or something, a kind that accumulated when a person was sad and didn't quite understand why. We were a couple, but Miranda always seemed to gesture toward the shed when she wanted something, like it was emotional leverage. I talked to Mr. Moss about it later: "Why do I stay with someone who wants to hurt me like this?" I imagined Mr. Moss saying back to me: "You don't know how hard it is, having a child." The words popped into my head like that. I wasn't sure about what they meant, but I was convinced that they were important.

On the day of the ostrich show, I knew that something was about to happen. The kids and their parents formed a small arc at the entrance to the ostrich enclosure. Miranda stood behind Jill, hands on the little girl's shoulders, very motherly, their eyes both big with ostrich pride, pride in me, the potential future father-figure for Jill, and for a moment the worry of being hurt was extinguished, as was the idea that Miranda was using me, blackmailing me into doing this, even; in any case, the eggs were right there in the center of the enclosure. All I had to do was go in, swing a stick at the mother until she backed off, grab a couple of the eggs, and bring them out of the enclosure to let the children rub—it was a bad idea, but I remembered these people were part of the ecosystem of child-brained idiots. They wanted my blood, if nothing else.

It was easy enough shooing the mother away from her eggs. Those big, black, cloudy wings poofed out in an arch; then she began her pathing around the enclosure edge, the children clucking their tongues and the parents clapping, no doubt making her more upset. I scooped up two big eggs from the nest and looked at the mother running around in circles. She kept swooping toward me, and I didn't know why an ostrich would be anyone's favorite animal. The ground was unsteady, and I felt myself moving faster, and I fell forward, my legs kicking out behind me. Looking up, to my surprise, the eggs were still intact, both of them standing upright in my hands, barely levitating above the ground in front of me. Blood poured from my nose. I imagined this was very exciting for everyone to see, the children especially. Then I felt her weight on my back, those enormous talons stabbing into me. The keepers flourished their sticks and backed the mother out, and I got out of the enclosure.

"Your back," I heard Miranda say. But I was busy with the eggs—I gave one to a keeper, who then proceeded to pass it along to one of the parents, and I knelt down in pain and showed Jill and the nearby children the off-white shell, rough and smooth at the same time, covered in dirt and shit, some of my blood. Jill winced as I pushed it onto her. "Hold it," I said, not understanding why she wouldn't hold it. "Your back," Miranda said again. "You're hurt. The egg has your blood on it." So I thought this was it, the end of the show; it was a good thing I wouldn't have to return the eggs.

I slowly began to try and distance myself from Mr. Moss. When I limped out to feed him, he hopped into the corner and watched me, waited for me to pour the food into his gigantic bowl. He never approached me. He hardly looked me in the eye. Sometimes I'd catch him scratching at the wall where there was a hole. He'd look out and scratch at the wall and hop over into the corner until I'd poured his food. When my back healed and I started walking better, I went back to the agency and worked longer hours again. I contemplated putting in to work with a talent agency specializing in film and theater. But I couldn't take my mind off Mr. Moss. I felt that whatever it was he did in the shed was not healthy. I knew it was not healthy to keep something locked up for so long. I had dreams, sometimes, of a house in the woods inhabited by my mother, and she'd been there so long that I'd forgotten her. In the dream when I finally went to visit, she'd vanished, her sheets a mess at the foot of the bed.

Eventually someone would find out Mr. Moss was staying in the shed. There would be a lot of shame thrown around about how I'd illegally kept the agency's property after having lied, and there was the issue that I might be considered cruel for keeping him locked up like that, which I wanted to blame on Miranda, but in truth I had no one to blame. I could have told Miranda off at the beginning, quit the agency, and rescued turtles, but I didn't. There was the issue of where to dispose of him; he was roughly the size of a child—if not bigger—and if anyone saw me carrying him out in a bag, there might be trouble. I gathered up my things: a crowbar, which I kept next to the bed in case there was a break-in; a large blanket, which I threw over my shoulder; and two or three black garbage bags, which would be used to transport Mr. Moss to wherever it was I planned to bury him. At the door, I listened to his sounds. This was the saddest part of it all, the moment before going into the shed, realizing that this was something I was capable of doing, that I had no qualms about doing it, that this animal whom I considered a friend was now more of an existential burden, and that I was willing to put him down over getting caught with him, the potential for the career end, etc. I hated myself.

I opened the door and he was gone. The hole where he'd been scratching must have gotten large enough for him to squeeze his angular body through. I went around the shed and tried to decipher where he'd run off to. My guess was toward the national forest. It was big enough, and we were fairly close, though he'd have to pass over a major highway to get into it. There was a chance he'd wind up backtracking and get caught in a residential area, which I didn't want to happen.

I might as well have killed him. I had planned to do it. I'd walked to the shed, contemplated doing it, opened the door. Now, I like to imagine him standing there, his back to the corner, eyes up at me: disarming me with his eyes, overtaking me, kicking me senseless, getting out of there one way or another, leaving one last mark.

BEAUTIFUL BIRD

I.

A genetically modified turkey came onto the porch with the intention of claiming me. Its green and purple feathers puffed out and shook, releasing a mind-numbing fragrance of lemons, blocking the neurological voice that yelled, *This bird belongs to somebody else.* Things had not been going well for me and Julia, emotionally. But still, I knew it wasn't right to keep the bird in the yard. I loaded it up to take it back to the turkey farm so it wouldn't get eaten by the coyotes that lived in the woods.

II.

The turkey knew something was wrong. The cab of my truck smelled of lemons. I couldn't think straight. How could I take something so wonderful away from the house when Julia was trying to spruce things up? The house was lonely. It was absent of love. Nothing would make the house happier than a scented turkey. On the road, I started to forget where I was. I nearly had to pull over. Then I remembered: I was taking the bird back so it wouldn't get eaten by coyotes.

III.

When I was a child, I wanted to be a coyote. They are like immigrants in the animal kingdom. I thought of my grandmother, who kept a white peacock in the yard. She kept its white feathers in a vase by the door. She did a cross stitching of the peacock, which hung over the mantel. She had porcelain birds, bird glassware, birds on plates, at the bottoms of cups, on the folds of shower curtains. Sometimes the peacock jumped onto the roof of the house and made calls into the open field. When the coyotes came into the yard and killed it, my grandmother wanted to get rid of all her bird things. My mother drove us to see her and take away some of the dishes. I remember planning to take one of its white feathers from the vase, but the whole thing was gone by the time we arrived. I once heard my grandmother say, "Don't ever rely on any one thing for happiness." And my mother once said to me, "Do whatever makes you happy."

IV.

I brought the turkey back; nobody had to know. Julia said to me: "You don't really want the bird. It wanted you to take it. They don't love you. They just want to be fed." But when it fanned its dust at Julia, she was head-over-heels in love. "Look at it," she said, covering her mouth with her hands. It was like she'd never seen anything like it before in her life. "Do you see it?" The bird strutted around in front of us.

V.

To keep the bird safe, I started taking shots at the coyotes. I'd never tried to hurt an animal before, but it felt like the lesser of two evils. I liked the moral conundrum of choosing between running over ten people or just one.

I would run over the one person to save the ten. One might say that quality overrides quantity, but quality itself is quantifiable. The quality of ten people put together should mathematically surpass that of only one person, but how am I to know what sort of quality the one person possesses? If I saw Hitler standing in the group of people, I might reconsider. I shot at the coyotes because the bird brought Julia and me quality of life that we did not have before. I didn't hit anything. They ran back into the dark, country woods, like coyotes do.

VI.

Julia went out and fed the turkey and watched it strut around in the grass. When it didn't shake out its lemon scent, Julia started holding it to her face, pressing her nose to its feathers. The turkey struggled to get away from her and hopped onto the roof of the house. I got a ladder and tried to get it down, but then I didn't know what to do, the bird was so heavy. Also, I was afraid of heights, even little heights, so I went back down. It only ever hopped down from the roof to eat, weary of human touch. Then it hopped back onto the roof and kneaded the shingles with its talons. Sometimes it fanned its scent across the yard, and we would go out and sniff the lemons and feel a moment of happiness.

VII.

Then the bird stopped fanning its scent altogether. I didn't know what to do. I'd given up on the idea of love or anything ever loving us or the world being a fair place. Julia said, "I don't know what I did. I don't know why it hates me. I don't know why God hates me." One day I saw her climb up onto the roof to get the bird down. It fanned its wings momentarily and hopped onto the chimney, out of reach, Julia flailing her arms out dangerously, carelessly.

VIII.

I came home from work one day to discover Julia lying on the kitchen floor, where she'd crawled to the phone. "I hit my head really bad," she said, and then she told me how she'd fallen from the roof. The bird had frightened her because she had frightened the bird. There was nobody around who could hear Julia's calls for help. On the way to the hospital, she moaned about a headache, a pressure, and she kept passing her hand in front of her eyes and slapping the side of her head and snapping her fingers. She lived another two days. She kept saying, "When I get home, I really want to watch *Madagascar*." She also kept saying, "*Madagascar* is my favorite movie."

IX.

I stopped firing at the coyotes in the field. They were just trying to live their lives, like everyone else. They rarely approached the house. When they did, there was nothing to be done about the bird anyway. There was nothing I could do either. The bird only ever sat up on the roof, out of reach.

LAST STAND OF THE ALLIGATOR KILLERS

A long time ago, our father cured Sharona of lupus with the blood of Astatula, the sacred alligator that lived in the blackest, loneliest bog in Crooked Basin. Me and Sharona were young, not even big enough to unearth a clam or grab a catfish. My sister's kidneys had failed. I watched her writhe on the couch the night our father came back from the hunt. Avery held her ankles while Father whispered and kept the hair out of her eyes. He drizzled Astatula's blood into her mouth from a tin can. Then something happened. She straightened her small body, and her head relaxed into the cushions. Avery let go of her legs. Father let the hair fall in her face. Sharona turned pale. Father did that smile he did when he was nervous. He looked at me and smiled and brushed the sweat from his forehead with a rag.

Vengeful horn-tailed Joes hissed from the water, gave us headaches, angry at Father for putting a bullet in their big shining goddess, for leaving them alone, for making the swamp a lonelier place than ever before.

Soon Sharona's ailment evaporated. She stopped grabbing at her sides and wailing. The hallucinations about animal genocides ended. An elder Joe could be heard sloshing around outside the house. I remember looking out my window into the darkness and seeing a pair of yellow eyes. Father's scaly hand pulled me away before letting down the blinds. And then there was a hurried splash. The sound of bullfrogs. I heard the Joes' alligator voices talking, cursing, saying terrible things about my family. Father stayed in the room to make sure I didn't listen, to make sure I didn't get up and go out there when they called. The night went on. Not much changed, except one day our father disappeared or died or whatever it is fathers do when they go out into the swamp and never come back. And then we were left with Avery, black-eyed and humorless. He promised to keep us safe from the horn-tailed Joes that came to our house occasionally to taunt us. And they did: catcalls to my sister, war cries to Avery, vows of vengeance, and to me, the promise that I would be a failure, that I'd ruin my family one day, eventually. They seemed to know this. I don't know about that. But they gave us more headaches, kept us from sleeping, kept us from ever feeling complete.

Years later, we are always fighting off the followers of Astatula's horn-tailed Joes, their skin bloody crimson, their tails spiked and laced with poison. Some have white eyes like ghosts and fist-sized nasal cavities that can track smells a mile away. The males have an extendable double-jointed jaw that leaps out of their pointed mouths, and the females hold theirs steadily open, attracting larger prey with a small, worm-like apparatus. You can drive a dagger into their skulls with the force of a jackhammer and barely break their tough-as-nails leather hide. Though bullets seem to do the trick.

I wake up and Uncle Avery is standing over me with the shotgun in his hand. Forehead sweat and bulging veins in the lamplight. The feathers on his neck are ruffled, which means he's irritated. He has tanned, scaly skin and a split lip from a fight he'd had with some merchant out in the swamp a few days ago. He doesn't look any friendlier today than he did then.

"Trouble," he says. "Joes are sneaking around out there. Broke in and got some chickens last night."

When Avery talks he has a voice like mud and sand. In the afternoons I don't mind his gruffness, though, because I like the quiet.

He wants to come off as mysterious, I think. It could be unintentional awkwardness developed during a life of quiet, cave-deep introspection, fairy-tale swamp living, sharing a bedroom with so many brothers, later only my stupid old father to really give him company, and now Sharona and me. I want him to seem more like our father, but I don't want to seem more like our father to him. In all our years together, he's never tried connecting with us, has never told a story longer than two sentences over dinner, has never splashed us with swamp water before going out on an alligator hunt.

I think it's about time I tell him to give me a little space in the mornings: Go shoot at the Joes yourself. You're a good shot, you're an adult. But I know this won't work.

I get dressed. I take my time. There's not really a hurry. We'll go out and shoot a few times, and then the day will get going in full.

Sharona bounces next to a window, pokes her head out and makes a series of incomprehensible noises. She listens for the voices of alligators and their mutated cousins, the Joes. Sharona has always been a little girl. She kept her baby teeth and her small-girl body, which might be some side effect of Astatula's blood. The Joes are getting back at us every time Sharona asks why she'll never be able to leave the swamp and go to school or join a caravan or get married. I think about her tininess occasionally, though I'm used to it. Today is one of those days.

"Don't see anything," she says. "Don't hear anything either."

"Being a bunch of smart asses," Avery says, hurrying to the table.

Avery gives me the rifle. He's confident that I'm next in a line of the big alligator hunters of Crooked Basin— there was my father before me, and all his brothers and sisters, all of whom are dead now except Avery; there are the alligator-toothed tribes up in Basin Proper who carry rifles bought off of merchants from Londo Vega, some from the Gknowles with withering, knotted heads like bulbous, powdery mushrooms—and I am supposed to be the kind of man who would become a man early in his life. Instead I have prepared myself to be the kind of man who will never become a man: for instance, today I remember stories of how Joes keep the bones of men in mud holes and mark their territory with tortoiseshell-decorated, sun-dried bodies. I think about how much better we'd be if we just left the swamp. I don't want to die. I don't want to see the rest of my family die. And today it seems there are much better ways of surviving than staying to fight. These are my thoughts today, and tomorrow I might feel differently. But for now I'll assume it's okay to be afraid.

Outside, a stork kicks a foot out of the water, splashing around for a fish. The stork growls, lunging its body into the water. The storks here are crazy. Sharona makes a little hoot in the back of her throat and bangs a wooden spoon against a pot in the kitchen. She bangs on things when she gets excited. Sharona might also be crazy. I wish she'd talk to me about her problems rather than act out whatever's bothering her.

And then she returns to normal. I don't hear the stork again. I pick at odd spiny things growing on my shoulders.

We watch the water. A Joe creeps around, searching for leftover chicken; I shoot, miss, and those that are hidden break out into the open toward us. It starts as a muddled roar as their heads appear from the overgrowth; then their bodies hit the water, and the muddled roar becomes a splash and gurgle. This all around the house, and the sound of Sharona banging something from inside, moaning.

I shoot one as it's crawling up on the planks toward Avery. The bullet penetrates its skull. This frenzies the others, which begin to thrash violently through the water.

Hive mind. They taste their own blood, which must be like a poison to them. They speak in words too quiet for untrained ears; Sharona tells us it's the stuff about animal genocide again. The turtles we eat, the fish, the dozing birds; they'll eat all the bullfrogs, numerous and easy to grab. They'll get at the chickens until there aren't any left in the swamp. They'll eat everything until we're forced into starvation. And they'll die trying.

"Just one said this? Which one?"

"I don't know," she says. "Some of them."

That's where I know I'm right; moving on seems for the best, but I don't know what will happen to us when we move on. Miles and miles of people who will take us in and never let us forget that we are refugees. I've met the kind of people Avery refers to, those visiting the swamps from cities and towns and villages. I want to like them, but I know they're capable of making you feel like you're less of a person.

I try to tell Sharona how I feel. Sharona doesn't care; now she's reading a magazine about knitting. And I have a feeling she's telling the truth about the animal genocide; I hear the alligators often, too, only at night when I'm super relaxed and hypersensitive to my surroundings. Always as my head squirms around on my pillow, swimming for sleep. Some nights their presence still gives me headaches. Some nights they make me want to gnaw my own fingers off. Some nights I can't sleep, the voices get so bad; others, like the time a Joe tried to emulate my father's voice and told me to come outside to find him in the swamp, I've trained myself to ignore.

Avery found that one hard to understand. He scratched his head at that story for a week.

One day I'll get Sharona out of here, and I'll find a way to make us safe. Avery or no Avery; he can stay here in the swamp as long as he wants.

Sharona sits on the plywood counter and dabs her face with makeup that Avery brought back from a swamp caravan. There's the off chance that younger boys will come through and ask Sharona to play. She applies dark red lipstick and puckers her lips.

I watch unintentionally, sometimes. It's hard not to notice. I don't think she minds though.

No, I watch because she is my sister and she is beautiful.

Avery chops the tail off the Joe we shot yesterday. It thrashes uncontrollably for a minute before coming to a halt. Salt is a thing we have a lot of, so there's not much else to do to make the meat taste less like swamp and more like cured caravan jerky.

Sharona goes out to see to the chickens. She talks to them occasionally. She tells me they say things like, *Perk up, little woman.* Avery spits on the floorboards.

Used to she'd talk to the chickens and Avery would watch her, an expressionless grimace on his face. I know he knows she's lonely. He noticed her doing it one time, talking to things that couldn't possibly be talking back; he looked at me, then sadly at the floor, and shook his head.

I wonder sometimes if Avery has ever talked to a chicken. I wonder what, aside from our father, Uncle Avery has ever been intimate with, whether he was ever a child at heart, whether I will ever feel comfortable crying in front of him, showing human emotion, letting him know about the state of my scales, how the swamp is slowly changing us for the worse, despite his occasional ramblings about how a thing is never changed when it is never moved and how this is best for everyone, the natural world especially.

I have big hands like my father. And I'm getting scales on the back of my neck: big, ugly pockmarks, which over time deflate and harden into a powdery white substance. I pulled three feathers off my upper arm this morning. I'll have to file my teeth down before long. All these things are unfortunate because the more I look like my father, the more my uncle thinks I'll become my father. The more tied I become to the Crooked Basin, the more I'll feel unacceptable once we've made our way out of the swamp.

He becomes upset when he sees me using fingernail clippers. "Bite them off," he says without looking.

He doesn't know I'm getting my feathers. He knows about the scales; he touched them when he noticed and gave me a nod of approval.

A few scraggly trees grow out of the swamp like moldy cotton swabs. Crows flutter over the horizon, and buzzards circle something dead. I count the chickens. We have a total of forty-seven in the good cages, stacked in a pyramid. My job today will be to mend the hole in one of the cages a Joe gnawed through. I've told Avery a hundred times we need to coat the wire in poison or put the chickens in closed boxes up on tables or suspend the cages by cables or build a proper henhouse with a latching door. I tell him now. He rubs the back of his head. He looks at the chicken cages. Then his eyes catch on the buzzards, and he maybe wonders what to do.

The wire nicks my hand. Blood drops down into the water, and I swear I think I see a pair of golden eyes looking back up at me.

"Maybe so," he says. "We'll get to work on that tomorrow. I'll get together some stuff, and we'll start some cage poles tomorrow."

Night again: a cage raking against a metal grating out there. My ears drum and expand at the sound. The wind comes into my room. And it carries the voice of a Joe: *I am watching. I am watching.*

Lone Joes come to my window often and whisper to me in my half sleep. They'll tell me sometimes they're actually a great big monster living in the water beneath the floorboards. They'll tell me, too, they're the ghost of an alligator killer who once hunted the basin. They'll tell me to kill my sister because she's the antichrist, a vast body of evil apparent in her stunted growth.

I know that this Joe won't take anything if I just ignore it—they want to be sneaky, don't want to be seen or heard when they're taking things like our farm animals. So when they speak, it's fine that I just listen. Just in case it's something important.

I am watching. I am watching.

"I hear you," I say, my voice barely audible beneath my arm. "You're watching, you're watching." They're watching. Which seems foreboding. Probably just a bluff for me to lose sleep over. So I won't shoot so well when they show up the next day to take our chickens.

A fly traps itself in my net. It buzzes frantically until I lean up and graze the net with my hand. I poke the fly out of the fly-sized opening, and it goes sailing off into the night through my window. Voice of the Joe goes silent as well, not even a little splash, the whoosh of water as its tail swishes it away.

I grill fish giblets for Sharona and myself. Avery is in the reeds hunting. He was having trouble getting his bowels going and thought it would be a good idea to go out and get some air.

I feel the presence of a Joe beneath the floorboards. Its slack body sloshes easily through the water. I get down and peek through the floorboards, and sure enough, it's there wading around like there's nothing wrong. It's alone, probably looking for something to eat or something we've lost that it can carry away.

I get back in my seat and look at Sharona. We eat the grilled giblets in silence. When she's finished, Sharona says, "I was reading in a book the other day that there's an advanced form of goblin crab that can reach into grottos and pull out whole bears. Their claws are exactly two feet wide but have the carrying capacity of a . . ."

"Sharona?"

"I can't remember all of it," she says.

"What else did you learn?"

"That in some towns everyone knows sign language because sometimes it's just good to be quiet. And sometimes it's easier to communicate at a distance using sign language. Because a lot of people just do better with the quiet."

"We'll have to learn sign language eventually," I say.

"Nope," she says. She stirs the leftovers on her plate around. She hasn't eaten the potatoes I roasted alongside the fish. She gives me this sly look. "That alligator hasn't said a word since it got here."

"It's a scout," I say. "It thinks it's being sneaky."

"Does that mean an attack?"

"It probably already knows we're alone."

"Do you think I need to wash the dishes before Uncle Avery comes back?"

"It doesn't matter," I say. I get up and take mine and Sharona's dishes to the sink, throw them in, food and all.

Today I'm feeling dissonant, less afraid than usual. I like the idea of being alone. I like the idea of Sharona maybe not bothering me too much, of the cages not needing mending, of the air not being humid, the crickets not being noisy.

Avery still hasn't returned. The Joe beneath our home still hasn't left. There's a knock at the door. When I answer I see a rough-looking man whose visible body is covered in black scales. He's painted some of the scales on his shoulder to represent the emblem of the Crooked Basin Merchant's Guild. His left eye is completely white. He gives me a piece of red material I recognize as the coif Avery wears when he's out hunting alligators.

"Do you want me to come in and tell you about it?" His voice has a jostled nervousness. You can tell that this one never makes house visits, that he only does business out in the swamp.

"Come in," I say. I think for just a moment about the Joe beneath our house, how it must be so pleased with itself, how it must be laughing into the firmament between its boney jowls.

"I saw you looking at that man a certain way," Sharona says.

"He looked funny. I've never seen anyone with so many scales."

"You shouldn't make fun of him. You should have been nicer."

Sharona hasn't cried since the man left. It hasn't hit her yet that Avery won't be coming home.

Sharona throws a doll up into the air. It hits the ceiling, comes back down, and she catches it. She has a blot of lipstick smeared over her lips, a spot of red coming over to the right.

"You going to read me a story?" I ask.

"I don't feel like reading a story," she says.

I sit at the foot of her bed, my back against the rod connecting the frame, the crisp, cold metal cutting into my spine. I think about what to do. "If anything happens," I say, "or I mean, if anything was about to happen, do you think we should free the chickens?"

I feel dissonant, but I've decided that today I'm being paranoid. Paranoid and lonely. Maybe something more. I barely feel anything for Avery. Except in my gut, a sort of tightening.

Sharona catches the doll. She throws it toward her closet. I know we have options. I know we won't have to run, and even if we did, the Joes'd follow us to the end of the Crooked Basin, till we run out of food. I imagine us drifting over the water in the old boat, the oar with teeth marks, slobber crusted on its handle, the alligators waiting for us to reach in for a turtle or frog, just waiting for us to put a bowl down into the torpid water for a drink, our fingers exposed, delicious and delicate. I think about the guns we have stashed all around the house, the ammunition Avery kept in a metal box on the floor by his little desk, and about his face that might have looked like my father's face, that I never looked at long enough, that I don't even have a picture of, that I really wished we had a picture of, just so that maybe I could look at it and feel less paranoid and lonely.

It hits me as I sit with the engine he'd been tinkering with: alone, alone, alone.

Wind blows. Reeds shift and spark, clouds open up and reveal blue sky, and the humidity comes full blast.

In the house Sharona is wrecking the living room; it's hit her now, too, how wrong everything is. I thought it was one of her occasional crazy spells at first, but then I saw it was sheer anger at the world, me included. So I sit with this stupid engine and try to make sense of my own anger. My feelings for Avery included; I wasn't supposed to miss him, but I do. I miss the opportunities we could have had, regret that I never convinced him to tell me more about his childhood, what things were like before they were alligator hunters. I miss his useless personality and the person who he could have been, that look he'd give me whenever I asked him a stupid question, like he was looking toward the sun and his eyes were so, so dry.

A Gknowle woman knocks at our door one morning with a bouquet of flowers in her hand. She's jet black, and her head is poofed out in the shape of a mushroom. It's the smoothest head I've ever seen, and she has these beautiful slick eyes, which maybe suggest sadness.

We invite her in to eat. She doesn't have scales; there's that about her. She's not like the others: she's not from here, and I can't say whether I trust her for shit. A tourist who heard something and means well and wants something in return for her kindness. She breathes heavily, and her mouth hangs open between bites. "Word travels around the basin," she says, forking a bite of gar into her mouth. "Says you got problems like your uncle died and now you're all alone."

"That's us," I say.

Sharona has manners at least. She keeps her elbows off the table and takes fragile bites. She also uses compliments like "nice head" when the stranger in mind has a particularly nice head. She says so now, and Glyn says thank you very much. It's very nice, but I can't figure out why she was so eager to come in here and eat our fish. She doesn't even know what kind of fish it is. Maybe she knows; maybe she's really from here. I don't know anything.

"So you planning on staying out here much longer?"

"No, I don't know," I say.

"What about you, sweetheart?"

Sharona says she doesn't care to leave, but that's only because she knows better than to trust a stranger. Could've heard about our uncle's death from just about anyone: a friend of a friend of the merchant who had broken the news to us, sure, but she could also be a junker, and we'd just as well be dead right now without any proper adults around to see to it that we don't screw anything up.

Glyn takes a look at Avery's red coif clinging snuggly on the bust of Abraham Lincoln just above the bookshelf full of plaster angels. "I need a place to stay," she says.

"Just for a night. Can I just stay one night?" Then she zips her lips. She has this look about her like she wants to say something but she's afraid to say it.

She watches me at night through the doorway, and I don't know if she knows that I know she's there. Sexy the way she props herself on one foot, her hands in her coat pockets. Her head is full of rusty-looking spores that glitter in the moonlight. Probably evil thoughts, too—ain't I too young for her?—she shifts a little and drifts into the dark. Later in the night I decide I want her. But I don't get up and go to her. It's just distracting enough to keep me awake and away from the thought of the Joes converging on us. I'm fine. I'm fine.

She has a handful of eggs. "I'll make us breakfast," she says. Mushrooms grow off her back, and she's developed a sort of hunch. Her eyes look foggier than before. I don't say anything about the eggs because I feel bad about her condition: she's not from here, and the swamp is beginning to take her. She's hazy with perspiration, too wet, too humid. A runaway.

So I think I know: She's come from the city, maybe joined a caravan, and ended up here in the swamp. She heard about our uncle. She's not from here, like I thought. So maybe she's just lonely. Her head twitches, and I'm afraid to ask.

Sharona takes me into the bedroom while Glyn scrambles the eggs.

"You see how many eggs she picked?"

"I saw," I say.

"Get rid of her."

"How?"

"Tell her to go away."

"But I don't know," I say.

"She smells awful," Sharona says. "Like farts."

We go back, and Glyn has spooned heaps of scrambled eggs onto our plates. Over breakfast she tells us that if we go with her, she'll get us jobs. The jobs wouldn't be glamorous by any means, but they'd get us out of Crooked Basin, and we wouldn't have to worry anymore. Sharona eats her eggs silently. I don't know what she's thinking. But I feel the situation has prospects.

At night Glyn comes to my doorway again. I think about what'll happen if we have sex. I'll have to deal with children then. And if we get out of here and I never see Glyn again, the lingering feeling of having unwanted swamp babies will always be on my mind.

I hear her lips crack. She stands there goblin-like in the dark. I don't even know if she can conceive, now, in her condition. If she doesn't get out of here, her mind might even become misshapen; that might even be what's happened to her, what's drawn her to me. She doesn't know any better.

I tell her what I think will make her go away: "We don't want to leave with you. I'm sorry." Kind of a half whisper so as to give importance to what I'm saying. It's not what I wanted to say, necessarily, but there's truth in it, and I think I'm happy with allowing myself to think about our condition a little longer.

She stands there a while, both her feet planted firmly on the creaking boards. Then she walks away, and I hear the couch straining.

In the morning she's gone. She left a note. *No eggs today. Gone to get some turtles. Will be back later. Think about it some more!*

By evening when she hasn't come back, Glyn's faintly yellow head phosphorous peels out over the reeds and becomes tangled in the wind. I let it slip that it may be Glyn, which sets Sharona off.

"What are you going to do?"

"What's there to do?"

"Are you gonna go get her?"

"How am I gonna get her?"

She kicks me on the shin and I wince. Sharona runs to the old boat shack and wraps herself in threads of rotting fishing net hanging from the ceiling. She doesn't cry but sulks, and I know it'll be a while before she untwines herself and returns to the house. I don't even bother telling her to be careful. I hate her sometimes. I hate the way she smells like salt and baby powder when she's upset. How the temperature in the room goes up ten degrees. How her brain has always been that same age. She might have some book smarts, but she's got the sense of a child.

Today I'm feeling regret, and I'm feeling that I want to hit something with my fists. Maybe even shoot at alligators to loosen up. I'm feeling angry at myself and everything. It's not a good feeling.

Taking inventory before I go out: the chickens are still alive, but half the egg-laying hens have dried up and won't lay. Running out of dried corn. Fishing supplies: crickets pile into the corner of the catch box, eating one another, or bound away before I can reach my hand in to separate them. There are a few cans of bait worms in the attic. Leather belts hang from the ceiling in Avery's room, so maybe we'll have to boil and eat those, before long.

I look at the engine again. Take the metal casing off the thing that has a big roller attached to it. Then there's the little motor that's powered by a hand crank, which I pull apart mechanically like I've done this before. I reassemble the parts, everything but the metal casing, which I leave for Sharona to wash with pipe cleaners.

Then the smell hits us: Glyn. Close enough to reek, maybe close enough for me to get to her without running into trouble.

We know the smell of a body. And I recall when me and Avery would be out on the airboat, and we'd see the buzzards circling, and we'd smell the body way before getting in close to see if it was somebody we knew.

The smell is so bad I don't feel there's much of a choice left. The sun's beating down, Sharona's cleaning the mess she made of the living room, and I'm putting on my overalls, packing some kerosene and matches, preparing myself for the nightmare. I take the shotgun.

I think about taking the boat and using a large stick in hand to pull me through the water, but I just know I'll get the stupid boat stuck somewhere, and then I'll be really screwed. So I dip down into the water and make my way toward the smell. A couple buzzards left overhead unaffected by the phosphorous. I come to the first island of reeds and step up. Feel something crawling down into my overalls. I keep the shotgun out in front of me in case there's a Joe hiding in there or a moccasin.

Glyn's body is splayed like a religious figure on a bank, with no hands and the head chewed up beyond recognition, but I know it's her. She's surrounded by fallen buzzards and myriad wildlife that'd gotten too close. Nearby there's a formless pod leading into a deep mud hole where a troupe of Joes lives. I take this slowly. The sight of Glyn's body is worse than the smell, but I pinch my nose close to protect myself from the poison. I drag her corpse up onto the bank and pour the kerosene. I light a match and throw it down, take a few steps back, and wait to make sure the fire keeps.

On the way back, I spot a Joe's thorny tail slipping into the water. I see its bubbles form as it wiggles itself away from me. I find myself wading toward it—the thing sliding across the muddy bottom like soap—with the shotgun pulled up, aiming at the bubbles. Then I blast away. It thrashes down in the water, emerges, and begins to run up on the bank away from me. I shoot again, this time stopping it for good.

While I am returning to the house: Sharona turns the couch over and finds Avery's pincushion, which he would occasionally poke with needles just to get his rocks off. She puts the pincushion on the mantel. Puts the broken picture of our father on the nightstand next to the recliner. Screws the knob back into the recliner, which keeps the recliner's back attached to the legs and unfolding mechanism. She boxes the busted television and drags it out to the dump pile that's getting surprisingly big now that Avery is gone. Looks out at the yellow phosphorous killing all the birds, hears the first gunshot, then the second, and worries about me.

I can't see any of this happening, but I imagine it. Sharona is a good person, and she is understanding, and she knows exactly when she's been wrong and that her anger problems are her own and that sometimes, even though I've lived with her all her life, I'm bound to misinterpret what she's saying as something more terrible than what she intended. Even so, I feel nervous approaching the house, the shotgun ready to fire at anything that comes toward me.

Then I see her sitting there on the dock, her feet dangling over in the water.

"What the hell are you doing?"

"What?"

"Get your feet out!" I struggle over toward her.

"So you can go around wherever you want, and I can't even put my feet in the water?"

"I have a gun. I know how to look where I'm going."

"Then what'd you do?"

"I took care of something. Go back inside."

"You can't tell me what to do!"

Standing there below her between her legs, I let my palm fly up into her face. She looks at me like she doesn't even know me. A kind of heavy breathing with her mouth hanging open. I know what's the right thing to say, and I try my best.

"Stay in the goddamn water then. Let the goddamn alligators get you."

I climb up onto the dock and walk into the house. The pincushion and picture of our father lie on the floor. The recliner is still dismantled. The busted television is still there on the wobbly entertainment center waiting to be boxed.

The voice comes back, just as I'm trying to sleep: *Going to drag your sister off and eat her arms.*

I roll over and think about Sharona in Avery's old room, which she's confiscated for her own. I get up and walk in there, look at her from the hallway. She's twirling a stuffed bear in her hand, balancing it on her palm, tossing it up to the ceiling and catching it on the way down. She looks over and sees me.

"What do you want?"

"You hear anything?" I ask.

"Didn't hear anything," she says. "Go away."

I go away. Not much else to say to her now. I hear her in there talking to the little bear. Then the door closes, and I listen through the night for the sound of ravenous Joes.

Chickens cry, wings flap, cages rattle, splash. I get up and get the shotgun, shoot the Joe that's there in the hall coming toward me. I start for Avery's room. The floorboards are wet, rivulets of water scraped over the wood by sharp claws. Sharona's door is open, the comforter and sheets tossed aside. She's nowhere inside.

I go out onto the dock and look around for her: to the right the Joes have made a pile in order to work themselves onto the dock, their bodies contorting and cracking. They're trying to tear through the chicken cages. I throw the barrel up and take a shot, and they scatter for a moment, and one takes a cage with it, the chicken balled up inside.

I yell out Sharona's name. I get to the boat and turn the crank, and it comes to life in a sputter. The Joes are down in the water, leaping up and snapping their extendable jaws at my ankles.

I speed out to the formless pod near where I found Glyn's body. This mud hole is ancient, black, and lonely with mosquitoes the size of footballs, rusted chicken-wire supports, waist-high water so thick and oily it might as well not be water at all. Sharona's not in there. But I hear something outside: there she is, running bloody over a bank, splashing through the jellied mud. Something off about her, something misshapen. She's crying. I intercept her and drag her to the airboat, and as I'm pulling her up I drop her, and she splashes in the water, the nub of her arm lifted, and I grab it and jerk her back up and hear the umph of her tiny voice.

She curls into a ball on the bottom of the airboat. Her hand is missing almost up to her elbow. She's turning pale. I get us back to the house and ignore the empty cages and broken electrical cords and electrocuted Joes floating in the water.

I lay Sharona on the table and get the iron going over the stove. I've tied a band around her arm to stop the bleeding, but I know I've got to hurry. The iron gets hot, and I hold her nub up to me and cauterize the nub. Her screams change something in my head. Something clicks, like I've just understood a new language for the first time. I don't see the swamp out there through the window but the boat and maybe the traders and oceanic caravans carrying remedies for infections and muscle spasms. Maybe a Gknowle who'll understand how close we'd come to getting out of here, how many times we could have left, and how little the rest of the world would care one way or the other.

Today I'm feeling nothing.

A stork lands in the water and gets electrocuted. I go out onto the dock and examine the damage: we've got no food except what's in the refrigerator and the lumpy stuff in cans. The fishing rod and equipment is all missing or gnawed in pieces. Dead things float all around in giblets. Something hisses out in the reeds, makes my neck tingle, and I go inside for Sharona, who's curled up on the couch, holding the peachy flesh of her arm just above the wound.

I stand at the window, keeping watch. The generator burns out, allowing the Joes to swim in and circle the house.

Sharona moans. I turn to her and she scratches her forearm.

"Are you okay?"

Sharona looks at me and stops scratching and rolls her eyes into the back of her head.

"I need to get you to a doctor," I say.

"You'll need to let the chickens go," she says.

I know she'll make it long enough to get her out of Crooked Basin; Avery told us one time about an uncle who cauterized the stumps of two freshly bitten-off legs and survived for a month in the wilderness before gangrene took him. And anyway, I imagine we're not even a day's ride from the nearest caravan. I'll bet there are doctors available. If not, all the caravans leave the basin eventually.

"Pack your stuff," I say. I hear myself. She can't pack her own things now. I'll pack her things myself. I'll have to take care of her for a while. Now I'm feeling afraid again, and I know this is normal. Maybe the boat will hold on, nothing will happen on the way, everything will be alright.

Now: on the airboat, doing something our father should have done a long time ago. I tell myself not to worry about what the others will think of us. Don't worry about appearances, the scales and feathers and pointed teeth, how strange we'll look and how rancid we'll smell. Sharona sits up, her injured arm tucked in her jacket. The wind hits her face, she squints, she's quiet. Tomorrow when we're in a caravan, I might feel different about everything. I'll probably be too nervous to make a decision, or maybe I'll regret leaving all our stuff and memories. I say goodbye to the swamp. Our house collapses from view, deteriorating as though it's fallen into a sinkhole.

BROTHER SWINE

I see something," Namwali told me. She sat at the edge of our dying snap bean patch, watching for new arrivals. My stepmother and I had taken turns looking for animals through a pair of naval binoculars.

"A pig, maybe." She adjusted the eyepiece. The purple feathers woven into her brown hair ruffled in the wind.

"Won't be him," I said, running my hands through the dry vines for a handful of pods. Of course, I doubted my stepbrother would return as a pig; people—especially young men who die fighting terrorism in the west, like Etgar—return as more desirable creatures, like birds.

Humans who deserve death return as things like pigs. Murderers, cannibals, etc. We often use these animals for meat when necessary.

We can only assume that by doing so, we're giving them a chance to die in the name of something good and maybe return as something more venerable.

"Etgar wouldn't come home to a village full of hungry folk in the form of a pig," I said. It had been weeks since the government trucks rolled into our village to deliver food and supplies, even longer since our gardens had tasted a drop of rain. But it occurred to me that Etgar wouldn't know our village had fallen on hard times, that its people were growing more impatient and thinner by the day.

I thought of little Donna's skin. Her ankles and wrists looked tightened and pale in the right light.

Namwali's mercury-blue wolf eyes lit on me. She turned and glassed the hill again, watched as the pig grew closer. I yanked out a handful of leathery pods that still had life in them.

"I see a horse," she said. "And a deer, I think. And something big is flying down toward the school."

Of course the eagle would become the center of the village's attention. I didn't need the binoculars to see it swoop down over the old schoolhouse. The eagle spiraled over the bare flagpole and caught the top, extended its wings, and gave a cry like a siren.

From the other side of the village, the tower bell rang. The bell rings once when food trucks are within sight, constantly when there is danger, and like a song when the Returned clear the pine stumps leading down the hill into the village.

I dropped the handful of pods into the bucket. "Should we get Donna and head up to the square?"

"Let your sister sleep," she said. "We have too much work to do, anyway." She referred to our hunt for food. Our going to the square almost weekly had become a fruitless routine. We had started to believe that Etgar, like my father, would never come home, not even for Helen.

I sat the bucket down. The spotted pig had already begun a line for our garden, grunting as it broke through the hawthorns my father had set out a year before his passing. The pig stopped in the weeds at the edge of our yard. Namwali abandoned the naval binoculars, used the stand to hold herself up. Her breathing quickened. She let go of the stand and dropped to her knees and held her stomach like something wanted to claw its way out. I stepped into the grass, and the pig waved its head and moaned, as though to say hello.

Namwali once asked, when we were young and jealous of the animals that came to live with us: "How often do I have to tell you the story of the man and the wolf?"

The wolf in the story was Namwali, who lived alone in the forest, ran into chicken coops at night and stole poultry from their owners.

I liked the lowness of her voice when she spoke of the man who had captured her.

"A man set a trap for me, in one chicken coop. He laid old carcasses on the floor, and when I came to steal a chicken, he released the wire door, and I was caught inside. The man said I had a begging look, and he had pity on me. He told me that if I would live with him and keep the other predators away, then he would spare me. He held a shotgun to my nose as he told me this. The very same gun we keep for a time when we may need it."

Donna, mine and Etgar's infant sister, kicked in her mother's dark arms. I thought that Donna had once been a field mouse because of the shape of her ears. Namwali fed her milk and continued:

"The man took me in, and I loved him, even as a wolf. We hunted vermin together. He kept my stomach full and my fur dry during the winter. I slept at the foot of his bed."

Namwali's wolf eyes drifted to the floor as she grew near the end of her story.

"Eventually I died as a wolf and came back as a girl. When I was old enough, I went to find him. I was sixteen when I gave birth to you, Etgar." Namwali looked glaze-eyed at her son when she came to the part about his birth. "When you were four and I was twenty, he died fighting a pack of vengeful wolves. I had you in my arms, and the wolves smelled my flesh, and I looked into their eyes. They let us live. I took the gun from your father's hands and shot the first wolf I saw. Then we headed south. A month later Benjamin took me in. He already had Straub," she said, looking at me. "That is all there is to say."

As years passed, Namwali's story disintegrated into a polished version of a broken summary: wolves attacked, the man shot, Namwali and Etgar lived, the end. It became a story she was no longer willing to tell. At the time, she had Etgar and me and my father, and eventually Donna. And after Donna, my father died, never returned to us, was never anywhere ever again. Eventually the fig tree, which Namwali firmly believed was my father reincarnated, no longer made fruit. During the winter, when she was curled beneath a blanket with Donna, no fire to keep them warm, Etgar and I contemplated going out to cut the tree down for firewood.

"He was your father," Etgar had snapped, passing me the axe. "Your decision."

I thought of my stepmother's hands, her feet, how she had always worried they might turn to ice and fall away. But when I considered how much she missed my father— how often she went out to sit beneath his branches, to look up at his leaves and dwindling fruit and pray and talk and laugh—I knew cutting down the tree would destroy her.

But I had to do it. Limb by limb, my father came down. I thought—maybe—he could have been made a tree to provide us warmth.

We nearly froze the winter after Donna was born. And when Etgar traveled west to fight and die and came home as a pig, it was the year of our village's starvation.

I could tell by the way Helen stumbled out of the car that she hadn't had anything to eat in days. She caught herself on the door handle. There were dark circles under her eyes. Maybe she had felt long nights, like us, imagining her fiancé's return.

She didn't speak to us, not even to Donna, who said hello and approached her with a typical child's nervous smile. Namwali jerked Donna back, gave her to me, and I put my hands on her shoulders and watched.

Helen squatted down on her haunches and looked under the boards of the house, as though she expected to find him in the dirt rooting. "Etgar," she called, her plastic bracelets jingling.

He ran around the house, squealing.

Helen took him by the cheeks and pecked his forehead with cracked lips. "Still have it," she said, throwing out her hand to show the pig a ring Etgar had given her before leaving. Her nose turned red and her eyes watered.

Namwali crossed her arms and shook her head. We had joked that Helen had been a well-groomed cocker spaniel before anything else. Now, Helen's dirty hair and broken nails were the opposite of groomed. And I couldn't watch her kiss the pig again, my brother or not.

"Be happy for Etgar," Namwali said, finally.

She never approved of my seeing Helen, after Etgar died fighting Californians. I took Helen to the movies, first. Both of us were awkward by nature with hardly anything to say to the other. And of course we were both ashamed. Sometimes, we held hands, and I would rub my thumb across her index finger. I never pushed for more.

When she came to the house to eat dinner, Donna would look at us across the plates of boiled potatoes and greens, and she would sneer, like she suspected something unspeakable was happening between us. Helen did touch my leg once, in front of Namwali. Under the table, her hand slipped to my upper leg and squeezed.

Eventually Helen really started to miss Etgar. She stopped pretending, stopped avoiding. She talked about him. Mostly about the good things—how they had floated in tubes down the creek, how when her car had engine trouble, Etgar would have it rumbling to life in no time. Helen thought he would find out about us if or when he returned. I didn't share her fear.

Through the window, I could hear his drum-like grunts. I cracked open the blinds. Helen opened the car door for Etgar, and he hopped in like a fat, spotted dog, crossed over to the passenger side, and waited for her to join before reaching his pig nose up and wetting her sandy elbow.

I tried to convince myself that it was not my brother. That it was someone else—a lonely con returned from the dead to take advantage of a random neighbor's generosity.

Donna watched out the window beside me, smiling.

"What's with the grin?" I asked, trying to sound complacent.

"I'm happy," she said. Her face had a weak stiffness to it.

Namwali came and rubbed my back after the car was halfway down the drive. I kept my nose to the blinds.

"You are my son, too, Straub."

I nodded, wondered if it would be safe to let Etgar ride the roads for hungry villagers to see.

"I don't know what to tell you," she said.

"We knew it would happen," I said, letting the blinds flop back against the windowpane.

"We knew, yes."

"Maybe they can work it out," I said, not wanting to argue. My thoughts irresponsibly returned to the way Helen's lips bent when she smiled, how one side was nearly always lopsided. Her closed, wet eyes. I hadn't seen that smile in a long time. Regardless of how happy she may have seemed to have him back, I didn't think the woman I adored would get on very well with a pig. Even if it really was Etgar.

My brother once said he began as a mole. It was the earliest thing he could remember—the warmth of wet soil, the quiet, sightless beginning not much different than that of a human child wrapped in its mother's womb. And eventually he was Etgar, a fat child in the arms of Namwali. On their own, for a while. When we were kids, he would mispronounce my name—called me "Straw," even up until the days when Helen came into the picture. He would grow to love girls, baseball, things that flew. Said one day, he'd be an eagle, and we all believed him because he was such a good kid, had led a good life.

"If I'm lucky, I'll be an albatross or a hawk," he said. Eagles were apparently hard to come by, and Etgar was a rationalist. Plus his mother never much believed in luck. She taught the three of us, after father died, that life was random and inconsistent.

"You could be a fox one life, an insect the next," was Namwali's eventually inevitable motto, and it stayed as such.

I began to wonder whether regression to animal-hood was really regression. Maybe it was ascension. Creatures that have never been human don't have much reason to worry, except about being eaten. Etgar seemed to want animal-hood enough. He never asked to be a leader. So I assumed being reborn as an albatross could have been a wonderful thing. But in my opinion, life was never random and inconsistent. I wonder if he wept when he realized he would be stuck to the ground in the form of a pig.

Etgar grunted, rutting his nose over the potato shavings Donna tossed into the dirt. "What else do you feed a pig?" she asked.

"Scraps from the market," Namwali said matter-of-factly, kneeling beside Etgar. She stroked his back. It was the first time she had touched her son since his return. She must have had her doubts too. But the pig did at least act like Etgar. And it seemed to like Helen, who had volunteered to go to the market and beg for scraps so we could spend time alone with our newly returned kin. Some vendors kept their spoiled produce in buckets for donations to returned loved ones. I wasn't sure that there would be scraps to spare, anymore.

Donna tossed out another handful of peelings. Etgar looked tired of the dry, wrinkled skins.

"I hope she doesn't let it slip," I said irritably, referring to Etgar's condition. Helen had agreed, before leaving, that she wouldn't confide information to those who were generous enough to hand over scraps.

Namwali stopped stroking Etgar. He grunted. Namwali stood up with me and crossed her arms and looked down at the scrawny pig burrowing its nose in the dirt. "The trucks will come, and things will progress," she said assuredly, wiping the dust from her son's back onto her skirt. She stuck a finger between her lips and chewed the nail. She was never one to resort to begging.

"It's been two months," I said. I didn't want Donna to hear. Obviously, my sister knew she was hungry and that a nine-year-old should weigh more than she weighed, but I didn't want Donna to suspect that anyone might attempt to butcher Etgar for meat. "You know they'll turn on pigs quicker than anything else."

"Do you know of anyone who keeps a pig?"

I thought about it. I couldn't remember any of the neighbors ever keeping a pig. Pigs hardly ever returned to our village for fear of being held for food. The droves who wandered into nearby fields with no direction were captured and never identified. If anything were ever to happen to our supplies, to the trucks or the little patches of gardens dotting the countryside, swine would be the first to go. Their bodies simply had more to offer.

Donna ran out of peelings. She bent over Etgar and gave him a squeeze. The pig reached up and pressed its nose against her collar. Etgar had rarely showed affection when he was human.

Namwali drew water into a pot and went inside to boil the snap beans. Helen appeared down the road, a bucket of scraps in one hand, a sack in the other. She sat the bucket on the porch and showed me the bag full of green apples. I didn't ask how she got them.

"I was followed," she said.

I glanced over her shoulder. Halfway down the path, a chimpanzee with arms long as it was tall stopped and looked toward us.

Namwali yelled out the kitchen window. She ran out onto the porch, iron skillet in hand, wolf eyes blazing. "Go on," she yelled, waving the skillet. "Shoo!"

"What do you think he wants?" Helen said.

"Probably just some food. We need to be more careful." I pressed the bag of apples against her stomach. "Put them in the cooler. We'll need them more than Etgar."

"You remember me," Donna said, scratching Etgar's wrinkly cranium. "D-O-N-N-A. Spell it in the dirt, like this." She got down on her haunches with a stick and scratched the letters into the dust. "Now you try," she said, shoving the stick into his mouth.

Etgar dropped the stick and put his nose into the dust, instead. He rooted and produced what seemed more like an ampersand than Donna's name.

"He'll learn," I said, noting how Donna's wrists had begun to resemble twigs. Communication with Etgar seemed trivial compared to keeping my sister alive and human.

Donna shoved Etgar's face in my direction. He squealed. "Straub," she said. "S-T-R-A-U-B. You try." She carved my name into the dust, this time with her middle finger. Etgar rooted his nose, making a circular pattern, and gave up.

"It's fine," I said.

He took off toward the shed and returned with a mouthful of straw from a withered pine sapling and sat it at my feet. He touched his nose to my ankle, and I bent over and picked the straw up, squeezed it, remembered the way he would mispronounce my name. No doubt in my mind, then. I knew this was my brother.

I gave Donna an apple, told her to eat as much as she could. "Don't get sick," I warned. "Eat. Don't look at me like that."

Etgar ate a mouthful of scraps from the bucket and started for the house, where Helen had prepared a pan of water to bathe him. "We'll need to keep him in, nights," she said. "The least we can do is keep him clean." I sat on the porch steps, let the straw fall from my fingers into the wind.

After our first kiss, I asked Helen what kind of bird she had been, how it had felt to fly.

"Wonderful," she had said. "I lived wherever I wanted. But I don't remember what kind of bird I was. If I was big or small. It didn't really matter to me at the time."

"Do you miss it?"

"I wanted to be human," she said, tapping a cigarette out on a rusted oil drum. She tossed the butt into a pile of empty water jugs, beer cans, cereal boxes. "People have it wrong, about being a bird. It's nothing special after you've been one a while. It's cold at night. You get tired of living in a tree and eating bugs. You have the whole sky to yourself, but there's never anywhere really to go." A pause. "And I couldn't find a mate, as a bird. I was bad at finding a mate."

I felt sweat beading on my hairline.

"What had you been?" she asked, which was a tough question because in truth I don't remember too much about my past self.

"I think I was someone else," I said. "I recall being very old. I kept a lot of books with me." But that was all. I was always so envious of those who could recall their pasts so vividly, though I learned to be thankful for the life I had now. But I kept a love for the smell of pages. That sensation stayed with me, I guess.

The chimpanzee made me think. I went into Namwali's closet and pulled the shotgun out from the corner, loaded it with the three shells hidden beneath the underwear in her top drawer. If the chimp came back—if anyone tried anything—we would be ready.

Helen was on the porch, knocking dust off Donna's skinny back.

"If you don't eat more, you'll dry up and blow away," Namwali scolded. They were all eating apples. Donna nibbled. Helen took small, slow bites. Namwali, smelling her apple, looked hungrily at Etgar.

He was tucked away by Helen's feet, his head wrapped around her bare toes. He didn't make a sound when he saw me, just stuck his ears up and blinked. I went inside to the cooler and spooned a handful of slop into a bowl and dropped it on the porch. He grunted and ate meticulously, as if he didn't want to offend Helen.

She looked wearily at me. I reached down and touched her hand, the one vein that bulged and turned blue, especially when she was afraid. She snatched her hand back and looked down at Etgar. Shook her head no.

Namwali took the shotgun from me and aimed down the path. "It's heavy," she said. "Much heavier than I remember." Donna covered her ears, expecting a shot.

I wrapped my arms around Namwali, rubbed her back. Felt the edge of her shoulder blades, counted her ribs. "We can't live off apples and water alone," she said, her eyes drifting again toward her son the pig.

"It's the wolf in her," I said. Etgar was asleep under Helen's cot in the living room. He hadn't tried to crawl into the cot with Helen but lay curled beneath, guarding her like a dog. "I'm afraid Namwali will snap if we're not careful. Just like a wolf. It's in her."

Helen leaned forward in the chair. Staring at the car, maybe, the moon reflecting onto the windshield above the wipers. She was probably thinking about getting away and taking Etgar with her.

"I don't think we should jump to conclusions." Her stomach rolled. "People think crazy when they're hungry."

"Etgar could have been anything but a pig," I said.

"Don't mention it."

Our voices were too low to wake anyone. I could hear Namwali snoring from her and Donna's bedroom. Donna always slept peacefully, curled under the thick cowhide blanket Etgar had bought with the money he earned hammering t-posts into the ground around our village. He did this before people stopped using money, started trading items instead. That world, surprisingly, hadn't been long ago.

"What do you think he did to deserve being a pig?" I asked.

Helen shook her head.

"Be honest."

"It's nothing," she said.

Prying information from Helen was the same as pulling the lid off a cement tomb. There was little doubt in my mind that Etgar had been good to her. I just wanted to be sure. If he had done anything questionable out west, we could never know. And Etgar would never be able to spell it out in the dust, not with the shape of his nose or the lack of attention he paid to Donna's attempts at re-teaching him the English language.

I put my hand on Helen's knee. It was exposed and dirty, poked out of her cutoff shorts like rocks covered in wax paper. She touched my hand then pulled hers back, got up, and went inside. I sat watching the empty chair rock, listened to the cot pressing beneath her weight, Etgar grunting and his hooves tapping along the floorboards, imagined him reaching up and touching his nose to her lips: *Good night.*

I crept into the house a few minutes later and saw a light flickering from Namwali and Donna's room. Donna's bony chest rose up and down beneath her cowhide, her breath rattling. Namwali was sitting up in bed, staring at the floor, a candle burning on the nightstand. Her purple feathers littered the floor. The feeling of wolf-hood never truly left her, she had told us before. I had always assumed the feathers were an attempt to forget what she had been. She must have yanked them out in her sleep. Now her hair was a strewn, greasy mess.

"I can draw you some water."

She shook her head.

I picked up the feathers and put them in her nightstand drawer, put her legs beneath the covers, and touched her forehead, half expecting a fever. "Try to sleep," I urged. Her skin felt normal. I blew the candle out, kissed her on the cheek, and went out in the hall and stood. Thirty minutes later, she hadn't moved.

I went to my bedroom—which had once been my father and Namwali's—threw off the blanket so I wouldn't be tangled in it when I heard the sound of Etgar squealing. I felt it coming, that night. But there was no way around it. Etgar would be our only way to survive, but the thought of Namwali eating her own son made me ill.

I lay awake as long as I could, listening to the sound of Helen moving around, muttering, probably looking in on Donna. I drifted off.

Early the next morning Namwali stood in the doorway with Donna, who looked skinnier than ever, her face dry, dirty and pale like Helen's knees.

"The snaps are gone. And the apples."

I got up to check. The beans we had poached and bagged and thrown into the bottom of the cooler were definitely gone. There hadn't been many, but they would have been enough for a few meals, maybe enough to wait on the trucks to come with more food.

Donna stood on her toes and shined a light down into the empty cooler. I walked out on the porch and went to the garden where Helen was fumbling through the snap vines, cursing and tripping over hardened clods of dirt, Etgar rooting by her ankles, looking up at Helen, back at me, back at Helen. The sound of locusts, a toad, a mockingbird waking and singing somewhere in the bushes down the path.

She looked at me and stopped. Yanked at the vines. Nothing. "That monkey was on the porch," she said, her voice hollow.

I shook my head, told her there was nothing we could do now.

"How long had that monkey been there," she mumbled.

I wondered whether the chimpanzee had seen Etgar. Maybe not—it had come only for the apples, found the beans as well.

Helen ran her fingers through her hair. "Can't believe a fucking monkey came in the house."

I went to her and put my hand on her elbow, my forehead on her shoulder. She stopped. Etgar was looking at me, watching us, and I wondered what he was thinking, what he suspected. I kissed Helen's neck, touched her face. She blushed and gently shrugged me away.

Etgar was her comfort. He watched, brushing against her bare calves. Embarrassed, I went back inside to Namwali.

Donna picked at the ants crawling in and out of a split in the window frame. "They taste like peppermint," she said. Nobody stopped her from eating the ants. Namwali was especially past the taboo of eating self-aware beings for survival—Namwali, in fact, had recently left to inquire about the nature of the food truck's lateness. Later she would inform us that other people and animals had gone to inquire too. Some had even set up tents outside the courthouse to wait.

Etgar watched us, his spotted flesh turning gray. Helen sat on the floor beside him, stroking his back. She still wore the engagement ring.

And I stroked Donna's back. Really, I was checking to see that she was not on a fast dive to deterioration. I knew ants wouldn't hold her. And one should not spend too much energy eating so little. My stomach rolled. I hated Etgar. For starving Donna and claiming Helen. He became to me the tree that was my father, something returned only to keep us warm and alive.

I went into the kitchen and took a knife and stuck it in the back of my pants. "Etgar," I called.

I heard his hooves clicking the floorboards. He followed me alone through the kitchen and out toward the garden. In the middle of the solemn vines, I knelt down and rubbed his head. He grunted.

"I haven't said much," I told him, "since you came back."

He looked at me. More Etgar than ever—the same eyes, it seemed, as the boy I grew up with. I wondered how it all worked, the science behind returning: whether the pig was born the exact moment of Etgar's death, how long it had taken him to remember, how simple life must have been before returning to our village.

"Why did you come here?"

He put his nose to the dirt.

"You shouldn't have come back," I said, thumbing his spine. I put my forehead down on his cranium. "I don't know what you did to deserve being a pig, but you know we still love you. And Helen's a good woman. I wish I—" *I wish I could have had her.* "But you were always good to her." I reached behind me for the knife. Etgar jerked, and I held on to his neck, and he squealed, and I pressed his back against my lap. I fell in the dirt on my ass. "Quit it," I said. "Donna is going to die. And you have to promise me that no matter how you return next, you'll come back to us again."

He stopped squirming, stopped squealing. I curled over and kissed him between the eyes. "Because you're my brother. You know that."

I thought he wanted me to do it. Maybe it had never occurred to him that Donna was starving. The blade was rested on his throat.

Helen screamed and was on me before I could do it. I felt ants crawling up my jeans, biting my thighs. Helen ran back into the house, Etgar curled like an infant in her arms. Donna's skinny figure stood in the doorway afterward, watching me squirm on the ground like a pig.

I pleaded with Helen and Donna that they would keep what I tried to do from Namwali. And I was ashamed of having ever suspected that my stepmother would be the first to resort to butchering Etgar. I told them as much.

I asked Helen for forgiveness. She said she understood it—she, too, was ashamed, but she understood. Donna wouldn't speak to me. I tried to feel her back again as she picked at the remaining ants on the windowsill, but she went to her and Namwali's room and lay on her mattress.

When Namwali came home, she asked if I would go to the garden and watch the Returned with her. This time there would be no snap beans to pick. I brought out the folding chairs, she the binoculars and stand.

"Braid me," she said, handing me a handful of dyed orange feathers and ties. She called out the names of animals as they appeared, slowly: "Ostrich." And: "I think maybe an armadillo."

"You can't see an armadillo from here," I said, my voice cracking.

As I worked on the third feather, her nostrils flared, ears twitching. She said she could see something weaving between the stumps, something large, something gray.

"What is it?"

She moved and I looked into the binoculars. A wolf, bigger than I'd seen in pictures, snapped at the legs of the ostrich. Wolves were absolutely never counted amongst the Returned. Namwali suggested it was because they rarely remembered—most stayed wild and vicious and could never be taught better. Her description of her past life, when we were children, had never amounted to this.

The ostrich made a dart for the village, and the wolf gave chase. The tower bell rang without pause, and as the wolf grew nearer there were gunshots.

The ostrich made its way to safety. The wolf slalomed through hawthorns and nettles, and the gunshots eventually drove it back to the hill and out of range. It weaved through the pine stumps and out of sight.

"Make sure Etgar stays in tonight."

I looked at Namwali. She had the eyepiece in her fingers, head tilted down to look, but her eyes were removed from the hill.

"What's happening?" I said.

Her face hovered next to the eyepiece. She looked at me and back toward the house and took up the binoculars.

"You think there'll be more?"

She rolled her shoulders. "Wolves always send one ahead of the pack." Then: "Maybe not," she said.

At night I brought the gun out to the porch, sat, and watched the path. I had heard about packs of wolves snatching smaller creatures—cats, lap dogs, vermin— from porches in neighboring villages even while the people sat with their animal kin, defenseless and afraid.

The memory in Namwali's eyes had been evident, but I was optimistic. Everyone slept, Helen with Etgar, and I could hear the vibration of Namwali's snoring through the screen door.

There was a breeze, the rattle of dead kudzu, and then a snap. I stood and heaved the gun up and waited for the light to emerge. Something walked around the corner, a lantern in hand. It stared at me under the porch light, stood like a human, wore a mining cap with the headlamp turned off. The chimpanzee, brave thing, had come back to steal from us again.

I flicked off the safety. "Go on," I said.

It waddled toward the car.

"I'm loaded with buckshot," I said. "Blow you in two."

The chimp turned, waddled on. The lamplight faded back around the corner. I could see a hint of its flash coming and going through the kudzu. Then it made a strangled hoot, and for a while there was silence.

The next morning Namwali asked Helen and me to follow her down the road to see what she had found on her way to the square. The chimp's insides were out in the open and chewed among a circle of wolf prints big as my hands; its arms splayed out like a human's, its fangs gnarled up at the sky, its eyes sunk into its skull. Helen vomited bile and Namwali held her up. I moved the chimp out of the road, into the brush away from sight. The headlamp and lantern lay in the weeds.

"I don't suppose we should risk eating it," I said.

Namwali's nostrils flared. She shook her head and rubbed Helen's back. It was already hot, and the smell was terrible.

Donna stayed in bed the rest of the day. We did what we could to keep her nourished—crushed spiders, picked wild onions from the grass and bugs from beneath the stones. She refused most of it. Namwali finally worked up the nerve to go into the village. It was late when she returned. She said there were more people in the square than the day before. They were still angry about the trucks and even more so about an invasion of wolves.

"I hope to never be a wolf again," she said. We had gotten lucky. One woman told Namwali that her grandson, a young ocelot, had been torn in half defending their home.

We would keep watch, that night—the wolves, Namwali said, might not attack humans, but Etgar needed to stay inside and away. We were all very tired and weak from hunger.

I showed Helen how to load the twelve-gauge—cram the shells in at the bottom, hold the button, and simultaneously pump. We would take turns watching from the porch in case the wolves came.

Namwali volunteered to go first. I sat in the dark living room with Helen, Etgar asleep in her lap. There was still plenty of meat on his bones. My wildness and hunger had thankfully vanished, or maybe it had only grown on me to the point of being unrecognizable. I wondered if Etgar would be too small even for the wolves, a waste of their organized effort.

Regardless, I wasn't sure if I trusted Namwali's opinion of what wolves were capable of. I told Helen as much:

"Maybe they won't come. Probably not. Definitely not." Nothing happened for an hour. We tried to rest. It was midnight before Namwali slapped open the screen door, waking Etgar, and told me to go out and watch for a while.

"How did it look?"

Etgar eased over the cot and jumped down to the floor.

"I think I can smell their scent," she said. Etgar trotted over to her, sniffed her feet, and went back. "I'm tired. And keep him off the damn floor."

Helen reached down and picked Etgar up again, put him in her lap.

I sat down in the rocking chair, shotgun in hand. I looked down the path. Something howled farther across the main road. Inside, Helen shifted on the cot. I practiced aiming the gun toward the crook in the path.

That's where they'd come. Had the chimp not been on the path the night before, they might have come then. But Namwali never indicated how real wolves would attack. She probably didn't remember, exactly.

If they came I knew it would be quick. I was afraid, more perhaps for my human kin than Etgar. I still loved him. I told myself this—a way to keep my eyes opened and my mind focused on the path, the darkness at the other side of it.

Helen came out and told me she was willing to take watch. It had gotten quiet.

"You should get some rest," she said. I offered her the gun. She took it from me without speaking, held it against her chest, leaned in, and kissed me on the lips.

I wished she would not have done it.

This was Etgar's fiancée. Had been with him for so long. I knew I had made a mistake. I didn't know how to say it so I didn't. I didn't know anything, anymore. Etgar was my brother. I hated my brother. But I loved him for remembering us, for never being a perfect human being, so imperfect that he came back as swine.

"Stay with him," she whispered, pointing to the door.

He lay on his side across her blanket, lifted up, and looked at me. I sat next to him. He didn't try to escape. I put my hand on his ribs and pretended to count.

"Don't know what we'll do," I said. I scratched behind his ear, leaned back against the wall, and nodded off.

Pop.

The gunshot brought me back to the dark living room, Etgar squirming and running out to Helen.

I tell everyone who asks that I don't remember the man I used to be: a lump of tobacco stuck between my lip and gums, a notebook flung over my knee, a pencil rolling over the cement, and pencil shavings crammed between the furls of my dirty khaki jeans. I remember that people used to stare. That I loved reading books—for whatever reason I can't remember. Now, every time I'm alone with a book, I fan the pages and smell, but I hardly ever read. Most recently I read a how-to article on cars and engines, which had belonged to Etgar. I read the labels on boxes the food trucks dumped into the square. Sometimes I helped sort them out according to the needs of the people who lived there, the animal kin they kept dear. There was nothing beautiful about words, anymore. Not on labels, nor included within instruction manuals, and our village doesn't have a library anymore. Those books were burned for warmth years ago.

I have often wondered why I came back as Straub—why, when all my life has amounted to is the care of Namwali; Helen, who barely looks at me; and Donna, who swears even today that being human is far worse than being insect.

If anyone asks me how being insect can be so wonderful, I give them a look and tell them there's no real responsibility. You eat and fly or crawl and hide. There is nothing painful about the life of an insect. And even such a short, minute existence must lead to transcendental possibility.

Etgar's life as a pig ended the night of the attack. Namwali hid Donna beneath some old tops and gowns in the closet. I ran out to catch my brother.

Helen was shouting at the wolves as they stole around the corner. One leapt onto the car, bursting out the windshield. One lay dead on the porch's steps. They circled around us and started for the porch but veered off when Helen made another shot.

Pop.

The gun almost flung her down, the scatter hitting nothing but dust. The wolves yelped and hollered. One braved over to the porch and snapped at her ankles. Before I could snag Etgar, he jumped down the steps and made for the wolves, squealed after them as though drawing their attention away from us. I screamed after him. My voice cracked, and my vision was like fire, all red.

Then the wolves were on him. Six of them. Snarling and pawing, tails flinging in the air. Namwali flew out onto the porch and jerked the shotgun from Helen and threw the barrel up.

Pop.

The scatter knocked two on their bellies, and the rest started up toward the main road. Namwali shucked the gun, pulled the trigger, and it clicked. The remaining injured wolves picked themselves up and limped out into the brush and disappeared. We ran out to get Etgar— chewed all over, clawed, a hole big as a fist torn into his throat by Namwali's shot. The wolf in her eyes expanded and ceased. Helen dropped down on her knees, put Etgar in her lap. Blood poured over her legs.

I covered my face with my hands. It was all I could do, all I could ever do. "Get Donna," Namwali said, pushing me away. I went back to the house to check on my sister, still crying beneath the mound of clothing in Namwali's closet.

This is how we passed the year of our starvation: cut up the remains, bagged and dropped them into the cooler for as long as we would need to wait on the trucks. A pig can feed a family for days. As I looked down into the cold at Etgar's remains, I reminded myself that this was not my brother but a pig. The real Etgar was somewhere else now. We wondered how he would return next. Whether he would come back to us at all. We thanked him for his gift of meat. Pan fried it in oil with a handful of wild onions.

We sat at the table, together, in silence. Helen opened her eyes to look. She touched my leg. Donna stared into space. Namwali, prodding her fork into the hot, pink ham, was the first to put it to her mouth.

RIDING THE WAVES
OF LEVIATHAN

Cecile Beach, third year of the Leviathan. My best friend, Tim, died trying to ride the tidal waves created by the beast. His younger brother, Elijah, had seen the whole thing unfold: first the beast's flight from the ocean, its multicolored fins the size of football fields, the spinal barbs like dead trees, then the splash. Elijah lost sight of Tim in the water near the lighthouse. He later found Tim among the rocks. Tim's head was split open, and blood poured onto the sand, and the water lapped up and washed it away.

Tim's death left me completely friendless. I sat around the house all day where I could play video games and read comics. I didn't imagine myself riding the waves anymore, any waves, natural or beast-made, and I certainly didn't imagine myself falling into place here with Elijah in Tim's bedroom, where we were looking through magazines and comics for something to talk about, something with the memory of Tim attached to it.

His board, the one with Gerry Lopez's signature on it, the one that Tim had ridden on his last day and that had survived the crashing waves, was missing from the corner. An armload of Elijah's clothes had taken its place.

"Board's in my room," Elijah said.

He looked at me solemnly. Elijah had taken the board off the beach as Tim's body was being carried away. I wanted to ask him where their father had been. Elijah and Tim's father, Charlie, was never anywhere to be seen. I understood the predicament completely.

In his own room, Elijah showed me Tim's board. It was yellow with two red stripes going down the center. *Lopez* was barely legible on the yellow, but it didn't matter; this was still Tim's board. This was, I felt, all we had left of him aside from the things in his room. None of those things really had memories associated with them. This board, though—this was the board that Tim rode to make me envy him, to know that he was the coolest guy I knew, that he wasn't afraid of anything. This was the board that made me love Tim.

Nevertheless, I said, "I don't know how you could have done it. Tim laying there like that."

"I didn't know what to do," he said.

"There was nothing you could do," I said. I felt stupid. I thought about the day Tim left to take his brother to see Leviathan. He'd said he wanted to show his brother something, and he needed to do it alone. He knew I'd have hated the idea. I wonder, now, if he'd still be alive had I intervened in some way—if I had known what he planned on doing.

Stupid, I told myself. Tim was stupid and irresponsible. He could have gotten Elijah killed, as well.

I went with Elijah to get the twins, Jessica and Isabel, and we pedaled to the beach and stood on the sand. We could hear the roar of Leviathan's fins pushing through the ocean and the rhythmic thumping of its heartbeat. It was a routine thing; the sound of its heartbeat meant we'd see it anytime now.

Isabel and Elijah went down to the sand near the lighthouse and threw rocks into the water. Elijah shouted for the beast to come out. I looked at Jessica, and she looked at me. I'd never had the chance to hang out with the twins, and I wanted to study their genetics, their mannerisms, but I was also too shy to look at Jessica for long.

Then, like a thing you'd sit and wait your whole
life to see, the beast, longer than a tarmac, fatter than
a clump of buildings, flew out of the ocean. It stayed in
the air a few seconds before crashing down. The ocean
sucked toward where the beast had landed and rushed
back out and caught up. The tsunami wave came toward
us. Elijah and Isabel ran back to the grass where we
stood. We watched as the ocean descended on the beach.
Trees and what was left of an old wooden fence were
shattered, and the beast disappeared, and the rhythmic
thunder of Leviathan's heartbeat continued. We could
hear it even after we had pedaled up the hill back into
the village. I had thought subconsciously that this would
be a moment I'd experience eventually and that me and
Elijah would know that everything was going to be okay,
that Tim's death had been a good one. But it was not
like that. We were silent and wet. The twins went home
without saying goodbye. The air was cold and the smell
of Leviathan was on us again. We smelled like the death
of the ocean and our town and everything.

The beast first appeared near our shores three years ago.
The heat of summer struck us numb, and those who saw
it first did not know if what they were seeing was real
or imaginary. The beast—it couldn't have been a whale,
must have been some kind of prehistoric animal, they
said—came with immense speed, capsized a company of
shrimping boats coming in to dock, and rose out of the
water, created those tidal waves for the first time, and we
knew we had a real problem.

Farther out, the beast crushed an oil rig, and the oil from
within made it so angry and lost, made it so crazy, and this
is why it stayed close to our shore, but who knows what
it's really doing, what it really wants? When Leviathan
splashed in the water, industries began to shut down, the
economy became afraid, and Cecile faced a blackout.

They said the rhythmic thumping in the air was the
vibrations from the whale's massive heart—what else
could it have been? My dad had to see the thing himself

in order to believe, too—and when he came home early in the morning, you'd have thought he had seen a ghost. He said that his career as a fisherman was over. He was done, he kept saying. Don't know what we'll do now, he said.

What this meant to me was that we'd be spending more time together. That perhaps with his lack of funds he wouldn't go out so much. None of this was true.

We were poor and underdeveloped, and now we had taken a step back. Cecile had not lost itself to people but to changing times, to the end of tourism and industry, to the waves that came ashore and toppled the weakest homes and centers when Leviathan was particularly angry. Killing the creature became a part-time business, but it sensed the danger, evaded, and came back with a force greater than before. Men died, boats were thrown ashore, women and children left the beach for good. People started to leave Cecile. Leaving was clearly the best thing for everyone.

I lived with my dad in a house that had turned green over the years. The porch had holes in it, and in the living room the carpet dipped in areas where the boards had rotted away. The shower didn't work, and when the tub was full of water, you came out smelling worse than before you had gone in. The good thing about the place was that the kitchen had never given us problems, the plumbing there was always ran, and the refrigerator was always full of food because I helped when I could to keep the thing stocked after Mom ran away.

Elijah started coming over to eat my teriyaki and fries, and this is where he told me about the magazines and comics Tim had kept in storage all around his room.

Now we sat together contemplating our next move. Elijah was completely serious about climbing into a tree and watching the twins through a window.

"Just like the movies," he said.

"You can hang there all night," I said. "I'm not climbing a tree to look at a couple of girls."

"I don't have no binoculars anyway," he said. He bit into a fry. I knew this kid was going to be real big in the hips someday, and he wouldn't be able to ride anymore. Elijah was already uncoordinated as well and slightly cross-eyed. Despite all this, he changed the mood of my house, my castle by the sea. The place smelled like scum and death and ocean spit, a thing you can never really adjust to, but I was laughing again. He told stupid jokes and talked about why he thought guys like us were into twins like Isabel and Jessica, the whole taboo element of incest, etc. Even so, I didn't want to go bird watching with his creepy ass.

We sat there and listened to the thunder of the ocean. The heartbeat of Leviathan was like clockwork around this time of the day. You heard the beat and you got off the beach immediately. You heard it and you thought about Tim and what he had been trying to do for Elijah—win his brother somehow, show him who was boss? Scare him to death? Say something about earning one's place? Tim didn't climb into trees to spy on girls. He never complained when he got turned down by anybody, especially not his dad. My dad had never even seen me get on the water before. I wanted to go out there and finish what Tim started. Even if he hadn't intended on starting anything, I felt the need to go out there and do something awful. And I knew if I did that, I could end up on the rocks as well.

Tim had been into skateboarding, too, but broke his ankle on a quarter pipe after coming off it the wrong way. Never rode that board again. He said his place was the ocean, his snapped ankle was a sign of his place in the world. He wore his hair back. He had a handful of coloring books under his bed (swore me to secrecy on this) because coloring in his bed at night kept him calm, let him think about life and what he was supposed to do with himself. He'd go to school with half the pages of his homework covered in purple and green.

Later we went into Elijah's room and read comic books. Elijah was reading, in fact—I just sat there, eyeing Tim's board over the pages of *Spider-Man*. I thought about taking Tim's board out again. It had survived Tim's death, had come back in one piece with just a few dings from landing on the rough beach, so that made it lucky, right? Leviathan was just an animal, I thought. An unusual animal that had never been seen or detected before a few years ago, and I for sure didn't know what it was capable of doing, but I was going to beat it this one time. Not with weaponry, nets, tranquilizer guns, but with bravery, with bottled-up fucklessness. Anything would do. I liked the idea of possibly dying out over the water.

Thinking Elijah wouldn't let me practice with Tim's board, I spent an hour and a half trying to replicate the feel of it with my own. I sliced the traction pad off and worked up a crick in my neck, cleaned the gunk away, waxed the back end, and wondered if the fact that my board was a foot shorter would really make a difference since I was really just going out there to warm up and rebuild my self-esteem. I took my board out west to Long Beach early the next morning and set my heart on some waves that'd be relatively simple for someone who'd lost touch with surfing. The place seemed safe, and there were very few Leviathan sightings here.

I'd eaten it on this beach a few times before. The place was a familiar sight, familiar water. The waves this time of the year averaged four to eleven feet, which would be nothing next to the building of a wave Leviathan would conjure up. But I needed to work on my balance, get my feet wet, wipe out a couple of times, feel the swell pull me out, get that initial feeling of abuse and death out of my system before there was something really at stake.

The sky was pretty clear. There was a little island out there, a hill basically, which I'd paddled out to before. I studied the shore, the waves coming up and popping the sand. The black rocks spread out all over the place, the backlash, the loneliness. I'd need to charge the shit, let it press me, work up my adrenaline. The waves looked to be around seven feet, which wasn't much to work with, and I'd have to paddle out farther than normal.

The water was cold, and the waves came at me, and I shivered when my crotch was finally drenched. That was when I knew I wasn't ready. I lay down on the board and paddled out. I went over the wave, each uphill struggle culminating in the threat of riding the waves at Cecile Beach.

I chipped into a couple lines before I was able to stay on the board. I walked up to the shore and wished I hadn't spent all night replicating Tim's board, and then I thought about the reef that was out there hidden in the shallows, how I could get hurt at any time, which wasn't very good because I needed to be fit for Leviathan, and I needed to have this sense of emotional recklessness, which I obviously wouldn't be able to capture if I couldn't stop worrying about some stupid reef.

At the end of the day I pedaled home with the board under my arm. I fell asleep on the porch with the board under the swing. It was late at night—or early in the morning—that Dad came home, walked up the steps, and shook the swing with me in it.

"Go inside," he said. He nudged the board with the toe of his boot. The mining cap was in his dirty hand.

"Where've you been?" I asked.

"Out. Charlie's. Long day."

He looked at me and rubbed his chin. He'd let his facial hair grow out. I never saw him go into the bathroom when he was home. You'd think he left the house to work, play, take care of things, then forgot his way back. I imagined him being awful at parties. Throwing up in kitchen sinks, talking about the days when he used to fish, when he could go out on the water and be himself and one with the ocean. I looked at him now and felt the presence of homelessness lingering over us. If Dad was anything like me, he was claustrophobic and didn't like staying down in a mine.

Leviathan's heartbeat woke me up just before dawn. I decided to stay on the swing and breathe the ocean, imagined my body turning green like the house, and then the drumbeats began again, tribal almost. I'd been dreaming about taking a math test with a bunch of adults in what appeared to be my dad's fishing boat when the beats started. I knew I was dead. I woke up and looked out a few streets over toward the road leading to the beach and the lighthouse near where Tim was killed.

Elijah woke up just before noon most days. He didn't go to school anymore—I don't know how he got away with this or what it meant for our town that nobody cared that the children didn't go to class. I wondered what would happen to Elijah one day around the time of his graduation. Our dads were working at the gold mine now; I figured if Leviathan didn't move on soon, we'd be stuck in the mine too.

A little after noon on a Saturday, I went out to get Elijah and ask him about Tim's board—just straight-up tell him, in fact, that I planned on taking it, possibly destroying it in the ocean.

He was a little surprised at first by my plan. He told me he wanted to see how well I could ride before giving me Tim's board. Then it occurred to me that Elijah had never seen me ride a wave, as Tim had never wanted him around because that's how it is with older brothers—*keep away, you little shit, this ain't for you.*

We took the board off the wall in Elijah's room, sat on the floor, and mounted it over our knees. I rubbed my hands over the wood and imagined waxing it one more time before heading out. And my father running out to the sand to watch me and yell my name. He'd tell me to come back and go home. He'd ground me and take away my video games and comic books. If I scared him enough, maybe he'd come home for a while, maybe he'd tell me why Mom had left him and me to fend for ourselves, and maybe he'd tell me about his day at work, let me make him some teriyaki.

"I'm ready," I assured Elijah. "You can trust me."

"I can't trust you for shit," he said. He rubbed the tail with his palm.

"I've surfed before. You just never saw me because you never came out."

A pause. "You don't know what it's like to lose a brother," he said.

"You don't know what it's like to lose your best friend," I said. Which I knew was the wrong thing to say.

He put his head down and started to cry. Silently, red faced. He got up and left the room and went to the bathroom. I always knew that Elijah was sensitive, did not take criticism well, but I felt awful anyway.

"Come on," I said, knocking on the door. "I know you guys were close. I shouldn't have said that."

"Go on—take the board," he said.

He was in there sobbing, probably sitting over the toilet reading one of those magazines their dad kept in the basket next to that dirty tub.

I took Tim's board to their little dingy living room and sat on the couch with it across my lap. I rubbed it with my palm, looking for Tim's blood, which I knew wasn't really on there. Had I seen Tim the day he went out with Elijah, I might not be doing this. I might not be risking Tim's board and my life and Elijah's sanity.

He came out of the bathroom and I heard him go to his room. The door shut and the bedsprings moaned.

I left the board on the couch and went home. Didn't want to see Elijah post-crying. Tim never cried as far as I know. He was a tough guy. Who cares, really?

I stood on the sand, listening to Leviathan's heartbeat. I thought about how I would get my dad out on the beach the moment I was on the water. Whether Elijah would be present this time too. Furthermore, how was I going to time the thing exactly right? Because you never really knew when in the evening Leviathan was going to strike. You could just feel it sometimes in the thunder of its heartbeats.

I went out a couple of mornings like this and studied the water. Tried to get a feel for how the beast made its appearance. The ocean was clear of boats and industry as far as the eye could see, an empty world of gray waves and streaks of light. It didn't take long before I could feel its presence and see its form emerging from the water like a mountainous submarine. It zipped through the water, and its tail fin slapped and sucked the water in, and then it pushed back out toward shore. The waves were unnaturally high, and I got wet and sat there on the sand regardless. My back hurt from where I'd tumbled backward.

I had second thoughts about sending myself into this doom. Mostly because being alive was an exciting thing despite all its awkward turns; I wanted to stay alive regardless, which was the point from the beginning. I kept telling myself that it was this—the surfing venture with the Leviathan—that was worth dying for because I didn't love anything more than the ocean and surfing. I pined for the water and the saltiness in my nose and the painful feeling of urination later. Dumb things I couldn't get off my mind that other people wouldn't understand, that I didn't care if they understood.

I caught my dad in the house about a week after talking to Elijah about using Tim's board. He was eating crackers from a box with tomato soup. He seemed like he was in a hurry. Had dirt all over his face and looked at me sidelong as he sipped some coffee.

"How's it going?" I asked him.

"Things are good," he said. He sipped the coffee. He ate a cracker and dipped it in the soup and ignored me sitting at the other side of the table now, my hands folded together.

"You're still working," I said.

"Phone still ringing?"

"It rang once earlier. I didn't answer."

"Then I'm working," he said. "Do the lights work?"

"I get it. I want to ask you something."

"Ask away."

"You ever hear from Mom?"

He shook his head, which was sincere enough. I'd always heard that you could watch the direction someone's eyes shoot to in order to know what they're thinking or whether they're lying. He looked at his coffee as he sipped.

"Whose fault was that?"

"Whose fault was what?"

"That Mom left."

He shrugged his shoulders. I'd heard from other guys at school how fathers could be in real life. A lot of them had moved on to better cities and better places, of course. They could afford to move and see the world and not live here and have to hear Leviathan's heartbeat.

Speaking of which, the heartbeats started right about then. Like a cement compactor but much slower, more vital sounding.

"She never calls anymore. That's why I ask."

"She never calls anymore because she's an asshole," he said. "She doesn't care about anything. Just don't worry about her."

That might have been true. I didn't know. I wasn't too concerned about Mom. I was more concerned about how much Dad cared about the subject of Mom.

"I'm going surfing when I get a chance," I said. "I thought you'd like to know that."

"To know you're going surfing."

"It's something I've been thinking about a lot lately. I was going to use Tim's board. I've been thinking about that."

"You're going to use Tim's board to surf," he said.

"Right out there where he died," I said. I pointed in the general direction of the lighthouse.

"Hmm," was all he could say. I didn't know what this meant.

"What?"

"When you going out there?" he asked.

I didn't know what to tell him. I was quiet. I sat there and rubbed my thumbs together.

The heartbeats went on. Dad was becoming visibly frustrated. His face reddened, and he got up and threw his coffee cup in the sink, which should have broken it, and then he slammed both palms into the cabinets hanging over the sides of the sink. "Goddamn noise," he said. He slammed his palms again and kicked at the cabinet below the sink. I hadn't seen him angry like this in a long time. "Never shuts up," he said. "That big fucking monster never shuts the goddamn hell up."

I continued to go out and study the heartbeat of Leviathan. A quickened pace meant it was moving swiftly; it often appeared above water when this happened, and it'd zip across and make a hearty wave ten or fifteen feet high. I tried to hone in on the times it'd jump. Rarely, it seemed, but the statistic wasn't impossible because when its heartbeat slowed and faded, then you'd know it was about to take flight. It'd go down to the bottom, then shoot itself up, and that's when the sound of the heartbeat would return and you'd see it fly out of the water like something that wasn't meant to be there or here on earth, or like something that should be stuck up in the sky with the moon. It was gray and had scales. Long, jagged teeth the size of skyscrapers curving and extending from an open mouth. The waves, when it splashed down, could be upward of twenty-five feet. Maybe taller. I don't know how tall waves can get.

Elijah brought Jessica and Isabel out to the beach, and we watched the ocean. The twins, with thick wrists and beautiful ankle bracelets, both had the same annoying laugh, but it was good to see their teeth again. They laughed when the water splashed them. I felt that the ocean meant nothing to them. Their presence created a mundane feeling. And it felt good to go and sit by them on the sand and listen to the heartbeat and watch the waves crack up and down. Occasionally we'd sense Leviathan stirring, feel the change in the thunder of its heartbeat. When it didn't take flight, and when the waves didn't rise up to a life-threatening level, we actually felt a little disappointed.

Jessica had a birthmark under her left ear. She asked if I had a staring problem. She smiled again. She walked home with me that night. We sat for a while on the porch and made out.

She had long black hair that I was interested in running my fingers through. I was afraid to do it at first. Jessica took my hand and put it on her breast, and then I knew it was okay to touch her. We stayed like this on the porch for a while. Felt alone there because the neighborhood was becoming a little more of a ghost neighborhood every month. And what was I supposed to do then when— her shirt off and exposed breasts, my hair a mess—Dad walked up on the porch, a blackness all over his face, his hair pulled back, the mining cap in hand.

"What are you doing?" he said. He flicked the headlight on and shined it at us. I put my hand up to block the light.

Jessica covered herself. She laughed a little and ran inside. Dad stayed on the porch with me, and he stood there against the porch rail with his feet crossed and a thumb in one of his pockets.

"Didn't know you'd be home this early," I said.

"Thought it'd be a good idea to come on home," he said.

"Sorry. I'll go inside."

"No, wait," he said.

He looked down at the warped boards of the porch and thought for a while about what he needed to say. His body wobbled around confusedly.

"You use protection," he said. "You're too young to put yourself in that situation. You know what I mean, I guess."

"I guess," I said.

"Damn," he said. "Damn. You need to watch out. You're too young for that. Too young to be messing around with some girl. You know damn well what happens. Damn well."

"Dad," I said.

He walked off the porch and stood out in the yard. I said his name again but he didn't respond. Then I went inside. He came back to the porch and went out of sight, and I heard the swing lurch, the chains groaning. I didn't hear the sound of Leviathan all night. Jessica lay by my side until around three in the morning and then got up.

She said she needed to go home, she was too young to be staying out with boys this late.

"It's dark out there," I said.

"It's dark in here, too," she said. In the dark I knew she was smiling her too-big smile.

We stopped on the porch, and on the left, Dad was still there in the swing, asleep. But he wasn't really asleep. He picked his head up off his arm and grunted, worked his way out of the swing, and stretched his arms. We watched him. Jessica, probably still a little embarrassed from earlier, crossed her arms and looked diagonally out at the yard into the real darkness, at the streets, weeds growing from between the cement slabs, anything but at the silhouette of my father.

"I'll take you home," he said.

"I'll walk with her," I said.

"I can go myself. I'm not a child," Jessica said.

Dad put on his mining cap. He became like a floating orb of light in the dark. He illuminated the yard and stepped off the porch.

"Alright," Jessica said. She turned and kissed me. She went off into the darkness with him, the only thing visible the beam of light moving along the street, and then even the beam disappeared, and there was nothing.

I worried about what kind of man my father was. Again, I wondered why my mother had left him. Honestly, he was a stranger to me. I wanted to kick myself—letting Jessica walk home with a complete stranger—I didn't know what to do. I sat in the living room for a while before he showed up, flopped himself down on the couch next to me, and threw his dirty boots up onto the coffee table.

"Just ran right inside, didn't even say thanks for the light," he said.

He sat down on the couch next to me. He nestled the mining cap in his lap and closed his eyes. His face was covered in dirty splotches. Ashy little spots where he'd been mining, then drinking, maybe fighting. I couldn't tell bruises from scars, scars from dirt. He looked strong. I know he'd taken a wave or two in his day—this is what I imagined a retired surfer looked like. His hands now, cracked, dry, were balled into fists on the edge of his knees. Then he snored.

Next afternoon, I came home to find a three-pack box of Lifestyle condoms sitting on my dresser. I went around the house looking for my dad, the box of condoms in my hand, my face blushing. I yelled his name, but he didn't answer. He'd come home to leave these in my room and left again. I threw them in the top of the closet where I'd probably never see them again.

I left notes all over the house, and they all said the same thing: *tomorrow, beach at 3pm, rain or sunshine. Be there if you want to see me ride.* I left one on the bathroom mirror and the wall of the tub. I left one on the refrigerator door and inside the fridge stuffed inside a case of beer. I put one of the sticky notes on top of his pillow. I worried Dad wouldn't see any of them.

I went over to Elijah's and asked if I could stay the night. Tomorrow was the big day. It felt right, and I felt ready.

"How many times have you practiced?" He looked at me and rubbed his little bald chin.

"I can ride," I said. "Besides, it doesn't matter if I stay on the board or not. It's not about staying on." In fact, I had a sudden craving to wipe out, taste the ocean, the water that had come from Leviathan. I thought at the very least if I came out of this with a broken arm, things would somehow be for the better.

I didn't sleep that night. I thought of Jessica holding me in the dark and tried to remember her number. I thought about waking Elijah up to ask him what Isabel's number was so I could get into contact with Jessica, but he looked peaceful in the bed. It started to rain outside. Great, I thought.

I wandered through the house and looked at all their things: pots and cooking equipment hanging off the old cabinets, trash and dishes stacked next to the kitchen sink. At their little dining room table there were beer cans lined and stacked against the wall. I picked up Charlie's mining cap and put it on my head and turned the light on. Charlie's wife, whatever her name was—there was a picture of her standing on top of a stack of magazines by the heater; she had been very lovely, blond-headed, and young—had never left intentionally but drowned in a pool on the mainland after a long night of drinking. Charlie, I suspect, never forgave himself for letting that happen. It didn't stop him from drinking, in any case.

Elijah had told me about the nightmares involving his mom. He barely remembered her really—there was just this vague memory of her holding him with Tim next to them, and part of this memory was probably all a dream anyway. Leviathan's heartbeat began, and I heard Elijah in his room yelling. He was trying to say something and was calling for Charlie.

I stood in his doorway and listened. It wasn't my business to wake him up, I told myself. *Thump, thump, thump*, went the heartbeats. And then he awoke, leaned up in bed, and rubbed his eyes. He saw me standing there and shielded his eyes from the headlamp's light. Lightning flashed and we both jumped.

"You're loud as hell when you dream. Could hear you through the rain."

"Fuck off," he said.

I said good night to him from the living room, then realized I hadn't asked for Isabel's number. Didn't care anymore. I took the headlamp off and tried again to sleep, the sound of Leviathan's heartbeat finally overcome by the rain and wind.

It was still raining in the morning. I stood out on Elijah's porch with my hands in my pockets, expecting Dad to show up at any time to get me, say I wasn't going out to the beach. Damn if it's not what I wanted to happen.

Come three in the afternoon, the rain was still pouring after a brief calm, the skies opened up and shut again, the wind blew, and the waves out there next to the lighthouse appeared mostly natural. We could not even hear Leviathan's heartbeat.

I thought this would be easy. Jessica held my hand. Elijah and Isabel sat on the sand over by the foot of the lighthouse. Elijah had his dad's mining cap on, and I'd dug one up for myself as well. It was strapped tight to my chin. We were all facing the ocean. There was no one on the steps behind us. No sound of a vehicle coming down the road.

Jessica squeezed my hand tightly. "Don't worry about your dad. Let's go," she said.

"If he doesn't come it might as well have not even happened," I said.

"That's what I said. Let's just go." She was practically having to shout through the beating rain. Her hair was down over her face, flat against her skin. Black and beautiful. I wanted to kiss her then. I touched her face, and she had thick skin. She flinched back, didn't like being touched like that. I was ready to go out there on the ocean, to do this thing for the fun and love of doing it.

"Where are you going?"

I pointed to the water. Tim's board was under my arm.

Elijah poked his head up and looked at me. He and Isabel stood up. Both of them had their arms crossed. Elijah shouted something, but I couldn't hear him.

Jessica said something, but I wasn't listening. I jumped into the water then, unaware of where Tim had been washed up, unaware of the rocks that had crushed his skull; they had probably been removed from the beach, not to protect more surfers but to keep the memory of his death at bay. They had probably been removed by his own father, Christ knows. There must be some reason fathers never come out of their holes. I paddled hard against the little waves the storm was making.

I got out pretty far, turned my body back toward them, and sat up on the board. My legs hung in the water. I looked around toward the horizon, which was brightly overcast.

Then it came—a bit later than usual, but the heartbeats began, vague against the beat of the wind on my ears. At first, I thought it was the weather, but then I realized it had a pattern and a direction. The sound moved around the ocean. It came so close to me that I thought I must be directly over it, that the ground below me was actually Leviathan. I looked down and the earth itself seemed to move.

I panicked and began to paddle back. My arms hurt. I felt like I was drowning right there on the board, my face in the wrong position, my back sort of hunched over defiantly, my body knowing it couldn't outswim Leviathan. I worried about Jessica standing on the shore. Her and Elijah and Isabel. I paddled for my life and theirs. I was going to get us out of here, and we were never going to come back to this beach again. Probably I would never surf again, this time for real. I didn't know anything. I kept telling myself that I didn't know anything.

And then it happened: the momentary silence—I sat up on my board, hunched forward, watched the beast taking flight, the closest I'd ever seen it, cracked teeth, horns atop its head, the multi-pupiled eyes—and then it landed. I turned, the sound of the ocean rolling toward me. I thought how fitting it must be to go the same way as Tim. I thought how special.

I stood on the board and kept my balance. I moved against the wave, and the wave pushed me toward home, and the lighthouse was just there getting so close, although I couldn't really see it. So close I was about to crash into it, I thought, and that's when I knew I needed to bail out. But a kind of free feeling rushed along my spine, my extended arms, and I didn't want to fall off the board. I didn't think about how shallow the water was here, how much it would hurt to bail and eat the coral and scallops down below. I thought about how good the rain and surf felt. The mining cap flew off, my hair whipped back to the side and cool against my skin. I felt naked and that nobody cared if I was naked. I was the only person in the world. Even Tim had ceased to exist—everything in the world that had ever mattered, my father and mother, whatever had become of them, that girl standing on the beach who I barely knew, and all the friends I had ever known who had moved on to different cities and better places—none of those things mattered. That's how death makes you feel, I guess.

Then the lighthouse was right there on top of me. I was in the water, my body tumbling against rocks and the rough plaster of the building. My leg became tangled in something. The ocean beat me back. I didn't struggle. Because this was it. I was ready for it to happen.

Elijah's hand grabbed me. He was under me in a second, grabbing at my leg. There was blood. I jerked my leg out on my own, and the pain reminded me of where I was, Elijah there in front of me—he hadn't even had time to take off that stupid mining cap. We looked at each other in the water. My vision was blurry. Elijah held me against him, and in his other hand he held on to the steps of the lighthouse. I wondered how I'd been thrown out this far. Also, I didn't know Elijah could swim so good.

My father didn't show up. Never came. I lay on the beach, my chest hurting, my head throbbing. I looked around for him. I guess he didn't believe me when I told him what I was going to do. Or maybe he did believe me, but knew there was nothing he could do about it. Maybe this had something to do with guilt. He didn't want to come because he didn't want to see me die. And my death would have been his fault since he had never been there to really protect me, and he just couldn't live with that, could he? I told myself this, anyway.

I had assumed, though, that he would be standing there on the beach at the last minute watching me. He'd jump out of his truck screaming my name, see me crash into the lighthouse, and then he'd see Elijah go in after me. I'm happy it didn't turn out that way. Because then that's what he'd have to think about every time he saw me. Tomorrow, I'll probably regret him not seeing me. My mind is constantly changing. There's no right or wrong answer. I will always be a stupid kid.

Tim's board, at least, broke into several pieces. It smacked into the lighthouse so hard that you can barely tell it was ever a surfboard. I keep a piece with me in the house now. It's out of sight, out of mind.

Jessica and I left Cecile a long time ago. Sometimes I look at our children and think about how I felt growing up. Maybe I should leave our kids alone. Let them grow up without me so they'll be stronger, more resilient people. Independent and clever, the kind of people who take risks. But I can't be that kind of father. That's the mistake I make, and this is my failing. We grow old together every day.

MOVEMENTS

Lately I'd been feeling stuffy in my head, so I made an appointment the same day Jodi was getting one of her prenatal checkups. The doctor jumped a little when he looked up my nose. He calmed himself and made that ah sound, wagging his flashlight left and right.

"What is it?" The pressure in my head was killing me. An odd warmth radiated from the middle of my nostrils. I felt something trying to push my eyeball out of its socket.

"I think you have a big spider crammed in your nasal cavity."

Then they were probing my right nostril so I could see what was up there on a television screen. He and the nurse went about it slowly because they didn't want to disturb the spider. I couldn't see its head, only two of its orange and brown legs, big and crablike, which curled slightly as the camera's light passed over. It looked like a tight squeeze in there.

"I've only ever seen this happen once or twice. Usually they get in there because someone fell asleep in a place they shouldn't have fallen asleep. Like on the ground in the jungle or in an attic. There was a woman I know who had been complaining about a severe burning in her nose. Turns out she had wads of baby tarantulas in all four of her sinus cavities. We had to coax them out with crickets."

He wiped his glasses. The nurse looked at the still image of the spider's legs on the television screen. She said that it looked really gross.

"It's in there really good," Dr. Parker said. "Your nasal cavity is barely big enough to hold it. That explains the pressure and why you can't breathe out of your nose and why sometimes you get that little tickle in your throat like you've got a rat's tail hanging in there. That's actually one of the spider's legs. This one in particular has some huge legs. I wouldn't be surprised if she let them stretch down your throat every so often."

I asked why he couldn't just pull it out. Get this thing right the hell out of me before something terrible happened. I was already stressed enough about Jodi and all her checkups. We were getting ready to have a baby, and spiders were supposed to be poisonous, right?

"I can't do it. She'd probably put up a fuss," he said. "God knows what this thing can do to the inside of your head. She'll use her fangs if we start yanking on her legs." The doctor seemed to know a lot about spiders. "They feel threatened like that. Chances are your body will push her out on its own, or she might just decide to leave someday. But for now her other legs, the ones we can't see, are probably all over the place, in your sinuses, everywhere. We'll schedule you for an x-ray, and I can refer you to a surgeon if you really want me to. I'll have to see about an anesthetic to knock her out without causing a fuss. That may take a while."

My father had gone through a similar infestation in his body not long after finding out my mother was pregnant with me. The situation was starting to sink in. All this time I thought I had sinusitis. I worried Jodi wouldn't want to come near me. That's how it was with my parents. I'd already started sleeping in the guest bedroom because I was scared of hurting the baby. My father's parasites would crawl out of his body into the sheets at night and pick their way into my mother's ears.

When I was born, my father avoided me. I don't remember a time when he was ever really there. I felt there might be some connection between parental absence and men's natural inclination for parasites.

"Jodi and I went to Thailand a year ago. You think I got it in Thailand?"

"I can't tell what kind of spider this is, so it's hard to tell. But since this one's so big, it must have been a baby when it got inside. I can't honestly say why these things happen. But I can say that you're healthy as an ox." He patted my knee. "You just need to rest and to know that this thing isn't going to hurt you in the meantime. If it didn't like being inside you, I'm sure it'd come right out."

The doctor made me an appointment for a CT scan. I was worried about my head and about what Jodi would say. Lying was an option. She was in her third trimester, and I didn't want to add any more stress to her life. But she'd find out later anyway. I'd have to explain myself, and then I'd be in trouble for keeping it a secret from her.

I'd imagined that her being pregnant would make me more nervous than the time before we considered taking that step, when I worried that she'd accidentally get knocked up and I'd have to change some part of my life that I wasn't ready to change. I'd also imagined I might be able to feel the fetus inside her swimming around, its legs doing bicycle kicks, its arms swatting at flies or insects. Being a father should have been something I became hopeful about. We made plans for the baby room. And then we started talking about school, which was too much. I didn't want to think too far ahead. I didn't want to think about anything. I wanted to sit on the couch and watch television.

Sometimes I wished our lives could have gone back to normal. She would lie awake at night, groan, vomit regularly and to the point that we both became concerned that maybe there was something wrong with the baby. She had prenatal checkups more than is probably normal. Everything came back fine every time, but I continued to worry that something might happen.

After learning that there was a huge spider stuck in my nasal cavity, things felt worse. What if, sometime when we were both asleep, Jodi accidentally breathed down my nose and irritated the spider? What if this was some kind of poisonous spider, aggressive, and could actually crawl out at night? What if it just decided to bite me from within? The possibility that I might be a shitty father, like Dad, bothered me, but the possibility that I might die was worse.

"I found your report in the trash," Jodi said, crossing her arms. She was sitting at the table, and I was spooning grits onto her plate. "*Spider in nasal cavity*," she said. "What's that mean? Do you have some kind of insect problem?"

Jodi was very supportive of my condition, like I'd been supportive of her when we found out she was pregnant. She made me a smoothie. She held my hand across the table. Of course she asked a hundred thousand questions. Like, how big was the spider, exactly? I told her I didn't know. "Probably pretty big," I said, holding up my hands about a foot apart.

"Can't you just blow it out?"

"Its legs are tangled in my sinuses, the doctor said."

"That's super nasty!" Jodi said and then asked whether I could feel it moving around and when I'd first noticed it. I couldn't remember when I'd first noticed it, but God yes I could feel it moving around sometimes, as if it were dreaming of foxholes and attics, prey wiggling in its webbing, little children chasing after it with stomping feet. I told her we were sort of even, now, in a way, because now I had a thing living inside me. She said, "You know we're not even close to being even. Yours is just a little spider. It can't kill you or anything."

"We don't know that," I said. I thought of its razor-sharp incisors or whatever spiders had that, when nudged the wrong way, could rip your nasal cavity a new asshole.

I told her about my appointment for a CT scan, and she asked to go with me. As the machine hummed around my head, I could feel the spider drumming its knuckles, contorting itself to escape the radiation. After I emerged from the machine, Jodi and I looked at the different layers of my cranium on a monitor, the reds and faded oranges of my flesh and tissue, the whites and faded yellows of my skull and teeth, the void of the spider. The spider's body, extraordinary even for a spider, was about the size of a squished lime, and its legs branched out in every direction to make the void look like the silhouette of a bush.

Jodi let go of her stomach and covered her mouth with both hands. I reached out to touch her elbow and she withdrew. Then she realized it was just me, her husband. She rubbed her forehead with the palm of her hand.

The technician printed off a couple of slides from my x-ray. Jodi put them in a folder and carried the folder out to the car under her arm. We didn't speak on the way home.

The next time we did speak, it was around lunchtime, and Jodi asked what I wanted to eat.

"I'll make sandwiches," I said.

"I'll do it," she said. "I was mean to you in the car today. I want to make up for it."

Later, after we'd cleared the sandwiches, I said, "Maybe it's nothing to worry about. We can expect to be rid of this thing any day now." I said "we" as if the spider were some kind of group project, like our baby.

"What if it dies in there or something? Won't you get an infection?"

"The doctor was surprised I hadn't taken an infection already," I said.

"How's it staying alive?"

We figured it must draw other insects into my nose at night, while I slept. And that made me question whether the thing created waste regularly and where all the waste fell. Didn't spiders shed their skin?

Jodi squinted like that was the worst thing she'd ever heard. "We have to keep it alive until the doctor takes it out."

"It's doing a fine job staying alive on its own," I said. "Whatever it's doing."

"But what if that's just a coincidence? The bug man came last week, and that's when you started complaining about your head hurting. That might be what's causing the headaches." We decided, sure, if the bug man had just come, then probably the house had fewer insects moving about, and there was less a chance that my spider could get the nutrients it needed from the outside. I didn't suggest to Jodi that maybe the spider was feeding off me, drinking my blood, releasing its filthy specimens down my throat.

"You know I wouldn't make it without you," I said.

"You say that all the time."

"I mean it all the time," I said. I watched her scratch her head.

Jodi couldn't help but tell her mother about my condition. Her mother told everyone else. Word got around that I had a special problem, and people started showing up at our house or calling to tell me about all the cases they'd heard about and that I'd be fine, that I wasn't alone. A millipede got into one woman's ear, stretched itself to the length of her cavernous flesh, and remained until she went for an examination with complaints about a persistent headache, visions of despair, crunching sounds, dreams of a giant millipede making a home out of an elephant's carcass. A man who lived on a farm noticed a lump under the skin on his shoulder, and another day the lump would be in a different location on a different appendage; the lump turned out to be a hissing cockroach, which had fallen into his side during a surgical procedure. A lot of the cases sounded more fictional than the rest, like the one about this man our neighbor knew who had unknowingly grown a fist-sized pumpkin in his stomach. If the pumpkin had grown to full size, it might have overwhelmed the man's insides and killed him. I couldn't find anything about the patient who had birthed a mess of tarantulas from her nasal cavities. I started to believe my doctor had made a story up to make me feel better, like everyone else.

I had a feeling I should call and ask my dad what to do about the spider. It was rare I ever talked to him.

Fuck him. I didn't want him to rub off on me or jinx my relationship with Jodi. But me and my dad had this connection now, and I thought it might be good enough reason to settle things with him, hear his voice, let him know I'm still alive.

"Right before you came into the world, I grew these lotus pods all over my skin," he said over the phone. "I even had one on my right nipple. You might remember I don't have a right nipple. That's because the surgeon had to cut it off."

"What did they feel like? Did they hurt?"

"It was difficult to wear clothing," Dad said. He was meticulous with his words, probably afraid to hurt my feelings. "Generally, it felt like a fire-and-ice packet strapped to my skin twenty-four seven. And these little seeds weren't really seeds but eggs. They hatched the most unusual scorpion you'd ever seen. They had two tails, one large and one small. I kept a few of them in a fish tank leftover from our first house. They got to be pretty big. I didn't water or take care of them. I wanted them to die. That's when I had all the lotus pod things surgically removed. I wasn't a very good host for the little bastards. That's around the time you were born."

I got to think I could make it through my spider problem. I thought about maybe feeding it with a pair of tweezers.

"Were you excited about being a dad?"

"Not particularly," he said. "But I know you know that already. It's why you never call, isn't it?" He laughed.

"Did you ever worry about killing me before I was born?"

"There were moments," he said. "I'm not in the mood to elaborate. I just didn't think I had control anymore."

"Lately I've been too afraid to even go near Jodi. Our child doesn't even have a name yet. Sometimes I just call it 'that thing' or 'the fetus.' It's sick. I feel gross. Anyway, I don't sleep with her any more. Not that it's any of your business."

"I had sex with your mother the whole nine months she was pregnant with you," Dad said. "You turned out okay."

"You never worried the scorpions would kill me?"

"Well, let's see. Let's say for the sake of argument that I was keeping two-tailed scorpions in the house while your mother carried you. Or even after, when you'd crawl around on the carpet, begging for milk. I never thought you'd die because you were the best thing that ever happened to me."

"Did you feel like your life was going to be over?"

"I guess every now and then I wanted to cut you out of her and throw you down a well. But that was just because your mother was so grumpy sometimes. She was a sweet woman though, as you already know."

That night I lay down with Jodi. I was tired and happy to be back in bed with her, our skin pressed together, the nuzzle of my crotch against her rear. She made a comfortable-Jodi bed giggle. Then the spider began to shuffle itself around in my head like it was trying to turn over. I could feel its legs curling forward and back along my nasal cavity, its malformed abdomen thrusting over and wiggling. I imagined holding a fuzzy spider the size of a lime in my hand, how angry it would become the harder I squeezed. I heard something scratching, like it was rubbing its little claws against a bone. "You hear that?" I asked once, my eyes wide, watering, scanning the dark for Jodi's form. I suddenly felt that being next to her like this was a bad idea, after all. For a while the spider stopped squirming around. I tried to relax. At around two in the morning it started again, and I didn't go back to sleep afterward.

"I tried. I'm sorry. I think it's trying to come out," I said the next morning.

Jodi, a little pissed that our first night together in a long time hadn't gone according to plan, sat on the other side of the table with her coffee and a book. "Welcome to my world," she said.

I thought about calling in sick I was so tired, but I wanted to hold on to the days I'd saved up in case of an actual emergency. I didn't feel the spider all day. I became unnaturally hot, probably from lack of sleep. At lunch I went into the bathroom and washed my face. A dead fly lay on its back behind the soap bottle. I picked up the fly and held my head back for a moment, thinking I might as well drop it down my nose, cram it in with my forefinger, but I caught a glimpse of myself in the mirror holding the fly above my contorted face and decided Jodi's idea of feeding the spider was silly. I wiped the sweat off my forehead and went back to work. I missed the feeling of breathing through my nose. I missed the smell of things.

That afternoon I called the doctor's office. The doctor was already out, so I asked the secretary for his number so I could maybe call him at home and beg for an appointment to have the spider removed. That was a no go, so I sat on the couch, watching Jodi listen to music on her computer for a while. She liked to put on headphones to shut me out. I think it's nicer to say she listened to music like this because she was trying to shut the world out, that it wasn't just me. The house, her pregnancy, the laundry I missed, the dishes I never cleaned. I was going to be a horrible father one way or the other. I thought about calling Dad again, but I didn't want to irritate him or make him think I only spoke to him because I needed something. Lack of sleep made me feel like everyone was irritated by me. I took my shirt off. I felt hot.

At night, my head spinning with the desire for sleep, the spider began its dance around in my head again. I could feel a couple of legs bicycle kicking in my throat. It became difficult to rest my head on the pillow. I gripped the headboard and telepathically begged the spider to stop. I beat my fists on the pillow and sat up. I heard something crunching.

Jodi made a hard breathing sound. "Just go away if you can't be still," she said, her voice muffled by the pillow and covers.

I got up dizzy and walked to the kitchen. Jodi kept my x-rays in the drawer next to the computer. I examined them for a moment and devised a plan for getting rid of the spider. I went to the refrigerator and stirred around for hot sauce. Then I thought about how painful flushing out the spider with hot sauce would be. I went to the bathroom and shuffled through the plastic bin Jodi kept under the sink, threw aside the plastic bottles, swabs, clippers, found the tweezers. I just did it, not even looking at the x-rays, a vague image of the spider's curled legs on the television screen in my mind's eye. The metal tips scraped against something that didn't feel like myself. My eyes watered. The tweezers jerked around in my hand, and I could feel the spider's legs curling violently against the roof of my nasal cavity. Blood poured down one of my fingers. I grabbed at what must have been its abdomen. Heard the crunching sound again, this time more determined, which tapered off in a slick bubbling that sounded like it was right in my ears. It had never been made clear to me whether the spider faced forward or backward. I took a hold of something new, squeezed moderately so as not to break it off, and slowly began to pull out a leg, big and scraggly, a slightly different variation of the color I'd seen on the television monitor.

The spider went crazy. I didn't want to stick the tweezers back up my nose again. I leaned my head over the sink and let a bioluminescent liquid pour out of my nose. I tore off some toilet paper and tried to blow. The legs in my throat tickled violently, made my eyes water. I pushed the tweezers up into my nose again and grabbed, yanked, let the spider shake and shift and the bioluminescent juice pour into the sink. I set this leg next to the other. I looked at the two legs wriggling next to my toothbrush.

"What are you doing?" Jodi asked. She stood in the doorway.

"Did I wake you up?"

"I have to pee," she said.

We looked at the spider legs on the sink. Jodi rubbed her face. Her neck broke out in a rash. She shook her head. I wanted to ask her what she wanted me to do. My head was killing me. The spider had stopped squirming, but now I had this terrible throbbing feeling, like maybe it'd bitten me. I told Jodi, in case I passed out and she needed to communicate this to the paramedics.

"That would serve you right," she said. "Jesus Christ. Why'd you do that?"

She pushed me out of the bathroom and locked the door. It hurt my feelings that Jodi could go on with her mundane little chores with two severed spider legs sitting on the rim of the sink like that. She came out and I hugged her. She pushed me away completely. "I'm still pissed. What the fuck were you thinking?"

"I was thinking I want to get some sleep so I can function. I want this spider out of me so it doesn't hurt either one of us. I'm just trying to help."

Jodi crawled under the sheets. "You think I don't lose enough sleep? You think it's easy for me?"

"No, that's not how I feel," I said. I meant it. I knew it wasn't easy for her, and I apologized for being impatient.

The spider was still there, but I was happy to be rid of part of it, to know how easy it would be to have the thing completely out of me, to be in control. I stroked our baby through Jodi's nightshirt. It bothered me that I never felt our baby kicking or its heart beating. Jodi would call me sometimes to let me know she felt a push. She said its movements felt like butterflies. I'd feel jealous. I didn't know what got me to this moment, but I held her as close to me as I could bear until she had to push me off. I'd pressed myself too hard against her and I didn't care. I felt like I didn't care about anything but being there against Jodi, drumming my fingers against her belly, waiting for the baby to drum back.

AN EXECUTION

When given the option to either crush the murderer's head with a rock or drown him in the river, I chose to drown him in the river. The decision had something to do with being in nature. Hearing the water running gently over the stones seemed like it might make things easier.

If I were to choose stoning, the Texas Department of Criminal Justice would have required that the execution take place at the Huntsville Unit in a cement room with no windows. If I chose the river, there was no way to tell what would be allowed or not allowed, but at least it would be done in the open air.

I'd been out at the river since my son died. He'd been hit in the head with a rock and then drowned. My visiting the river several times was of growing concern to the people in my family. My brother, of all people, was the one to finally speak up at the end of Thanksgiving: "You're so fucking depressing. We can't take it anymore. If you go out there again, I'm going to come over to your trailer and kick your ass. What are you all looking at? You're all thinking it!"

My ex-wife, who no one knew was my ex-wife yet, asked to speak with him in private. I think she gave him an earful. She still cared about me, but statistically couples do not stay together after the death of a child.

My brother had always been an asshole, but he was right: I needed to move on, but the coming execution made it impossible.

My son was with Ellis, the murderer, at the river. They had been taking a bath. This was during the spring. They'd been living in and out of tents for months at different national parks. A friend had given them a truck.

He and Ellis just hit it off. It's unclear whether they were in a relationship. I never thought to ask—not that we ever spoke anyway. There was no motive behind Ellis's attack. He turned himself in soon after murdering my son.

Russ was found three days after his murder, near a paper mill. His body, in addition to having bloated from being in the river, had absorbed pollutants from the mill and had taken on a sort of dark hue around his bonier features, cheeks I'd always thought looked like my mother's cheeks.

The friend who'd loaned them the truck claimed there was nothing unusual about Ellis. He described him to me thusly: "He had a tic. Constantly looking around as if in awe of something. There's a lot of trees around here. Pine. I don't know what he could have been in awe of. I don't know why he murdered Russel. They'd seemed fine. One would talk, wait for the other to speak, then talk again. They were polite and thankful for the truck. I would have loaned Russel a truck any day of the week. I hope you get to splatter the fucker's brains out."

The truck had been abandoned in a Chevron parking lot three miles from the spot where Russ was bludgeoned and drowned. Indicating Ellis didn't care if he was caught—being mobile, though, I figured he would have gotten as far from the area as possible.

I've tried to analyze certain features of the murder. For instance, Ellis's indication of the murder location and the body's location was inconsistent—obviously, he'd dragged my son's body from the river after changing his mind about letting it float to the ocean. Again, this indicates some form of remorse, which I can appreciate given the circumstances. I've been more reasonable about this whole thing than I should be, and that's perhaps one of the reasons why my ex-wife left me: I was very fucking weird, but human, probably.

In truth, when I went down to the river where my son was murdered, it wasn't to brood or try to connect with the universe in some obscure way that only the parents of murdered children understand. It's just that I'd gone down once to see where he'd been drowned, and I couldn't help myself: it was a nice place, and I liked being there.

I went down to the water and felt the rocks against my bare feet, and the only thing I was thinking was here I am in this river, letting the water run over my feet, and over there are a couple of people sitting in folding chairs, looking at an opening in the trees where a great big bear had been spotted some months before.

It was missing the vista of a mountain against a slab of dark green; the silhouette of buildings peeked beyond a thick layer of trees. Otherwise, it was a normal-enough river, and I promised myself to come back often.

It was good being the father of a murdered son. I could stand out here by the river without feeling bad about it. I could miss my job as a lift operator occasionally, saying "I don't think today's the best day to operate a lift" or some such excuse, and my boss, being reasonable and having lost a son of his own (not murder related), would tell me to take a couple of days and get my mind back in order.

The TDCJ, however, specified that the execution river would in fact be designated by the department and would not be the river where Russ was drowned. The designated river went through a gated section of land. They'd put out a net across the stretch of the river in case Ellis tried to get away.

"That's great," I said, referring to the location. "I was worried you'd just give me a bucket of water to drown him in."

The woman on the phone didn't laugh. It's important that I say she didn't laugh because a lot of people laughed at my jokes lately, my lawyers especially, even when the jokes weren't funny. It was good to be held accountable for my awkward behavior—I told a joke about a bucket and drowning that was not funny and was in no way deserving of a laugh, and like magic, she did not laugh. Just like things used to be before my son was murdered at the river.

She sent a list of rules I was to follow regarding the execution:

1.) You will provide an impact statement upon arrival at the river. Before and after the impact statement, all parties shall remain silent.

2.) While you are present in the company of the guilty party, you shall not respond to anything E. THURMAN says.

3.) You may put your hands around the guilty party's throat, if you wish.

4.) While the guilty party will be restrained, you may still feel threatened; if this is the case, you may provide a hand signal to the constable.

5.) You may not speak to any members of the press who may be present at the execution itself, but you are free to speak to the press after the constable has called the guilty party's time of death.

Number four frightened me. I'd never felt scared of the man who had killed my son. But now something felt different: like he was out in my yard, waiting for me to step out for a cigarette.

The trailer's door was locked. I went into the den and closed the curtains. I listened for the sound of the gravel road, afterward, and for the cries of the dog next door that always barked at every little thing that passed by.

Fears aside, it was really amazing that I was going to participate in an execution. I have really good lawyers. One in five executions are performed by the state behind closed doors. Really good lawyers, though, can put your finger on the trigger.

Although I'll admit that I didn't want to do it. My lawyers talked me into doing it. "Getting revenge on Ellis would be better than years of therapy," they said.

The truth is I couldn't afford these lawyers. They were loaned to me by the state. This was made possible because of how my son was found: three kids, all under the age of nine, had been playing on the outskirts of the paper mill and found him in the rocks looking like a bloated summer sausage. They were all in therapy now, and a big conversation had started as a result about the intricacies of childhood and death. That gave the case a lot of attention, and the state thought, well, why the hell not, let's give this poor fucker a chance to avenge his son, and perhaps one of us will be reelected.

My brother came to stay the night at the trailer. We drank together. We took our jackets off and smoked pot and drank and listened to 80s rock music. We slammed vodka late into the night and gave each other high fives. I thought very hard in my drunken stupor about the possibility of going back to school someday and going into law somehow. I told my brother about possibly going back to school to become a lawyer, and he just sat quietly, rotating the glass in his hands.

In the morning we went to go find something to eat. He felt bad about giving me shit the other day. That's life, though, I said. We ate at a little backroad diner with hamburgers and chicken strips. I ordered the chicken. He asked how I was doing.

"I made a garden. I have cabbage growing in a box off the ground about like—" I showed him the size of the box with my hands.

"Cabbage," he said.

"It doesn't stalk. Bloom. It doesn't—"

"I don't know what cabbage does or doesn't do," he said, noncommittally.

Toward the end of our talking about cabbage, he got up to go to the bathroom. The waitress came by and asked if I wanted another coffee.

The more coffee I drank, the more anxious I became: I worried about the murderer and his unlikely appearance before me at night at the foot of my bed to strangle me or kill me with a rock. I already considered these things often, but coffee made it worse.

My ex-wife said I should start drinking tea. But I just couldn't get into tea, so I continued drinking coffee.

When I met my ex-wife for dinner one evening, she asked me a lot of the same questions as my brother: How are you doing? What have you been up to? Are you holding it together?

Sometimes my ex-wife and I would hook up at a motel. Sex was still fresh on our minds even if romance was out of the question. We were both single, and there were no strings attached aside from the emotional baggage of having to be alone after hooking up—and she would always bring forth the topic of how we couldn't keep doing this, even though she was smiling when she said it and we both knew that so long as we were both single, this would probably keep happening.

But realistically, we were both fighting something that neither of us was equipped for—she was angry she didn't get to take place in the execution. It had fallen on me for gender reasons. That's what my lawyers told me. It didn't make sense, but I don't think a lot of anything makes any sense. We had sex, and then we left, and I knew I'd hear from her again at some point.

It was difficult writing a second impact statement. I didn't know what else to say about my son. I didn't know what to say about the murderer, either. Everyone, including the murderer, already knew that what had happened was wrong, that I was feeling bad, would always feel bad, and so I didn't see the point in going through with this again. I'd already given a brief statement during the hearing; that had taken me a week to write.

"Well," the woman told me over the phone, "this is a separate thing. The post-sentencing statement. You can say whatever you want."

"I'll keep it short."

"You might have your lawyers work on it with you. They can do that."

This part of the judicial process has always intrigued me. I'm a somewhat literate person, but I've seen court cases where people who'd probably never written a word in their lives were asked to pen this monumental, passionate thing, which frankly must be difficult for any professional writer to come up with, particularly when they're in a state of emotional turmoil. But I didn't want my lawyers to do it; they were good people, but I didn't want them to have to write anything for me.

I couldn't even remember what I'd said in my previous impact statement. I thought I might could go back and look at the Notepad file and see if I could salvage anything from that.

I started talking to animals after the death of my son. I had full conversations with the creatures that took shelter under my trailer. You know how possums are— they stop and look at you, and they don't get in a big hurry to run away or anything, so they're exciting to talk to about life, etc. I asked about her possum family. I wanted to see those baby possums hanging off her like a possum coat. In addition to the possum, I talked financial advice over with the cat. I got into fights with the cat too. There was a huge bat population in the trailer park, but they wouldn't sit still long enough to talk to. You never knew where they'd fly—they'd zip through the air, and I'd catch a glimpse of them making an arc beneath the orange light, and then they'd be gone. They reminded me of growing up in an apartment with my mother in Hammond—waiting for her to come home, the bats swooping down to catch the bugs that clouded the lights of the apartment's swimming pool.

Neighbors came to congratulate me on the execution. They'd say things like "make it last" and "I wish you" this or that, all that crap they didn't really mean.

I nodded and smiled; despite my shyness about all the attention, it still felt like a powerful position to be in, and I'd tried for a long time already, even before the murder of my son, to be okay with his loss—he'd been long gone. Part of me had gone with him. This was even before he'd said goodbye—he'd gone to high school, and a part of me had simply left the house and didn't come back. I think it was the part of me that liked cooking and tasting: a good bit of the spirit of the kitchen had simply vanished.

One of the neighbors had an unusual request: she wanted me to gouge the murderer's eyes out with my thumbs as I held him under the water. I showed her the rules and explained that it would be a bad idea if I gouged the murderer's eyes out with my thumbs since it only specified putting my hands around his throat. She went on to explain that I could hold him under the water and do it out of sight of the guard who would be there with us, but I couldn't help but think that this was still a human being, and if it weren't for this woman telling me to do something horrible to the man's eyes, I might not have considered the fact that for whatever reason, the murder of my son must have been some kind of fluke, that had circumstances not aligned just so, he might still be alive, and he and E THURMAN might still have been able to get through the spring. He might have come home to say, "Dad, I want you to meet someone." That kind of thing crossed my mind.

My brother came to see me again. He'd been coming to see me a lot lately; this was fine. He asked if I'd been down to the river.

No, I'd not been down to the river, I told him.

He seemed glad of this. But he wanted to talk to me about something. I wasn't sure what his problem was. He always looked like an angry individual. He had big thumbs and knuckles, and he was always scratching his chin with his fingers.

Then he told me about my son—something he knew that he thought I should know about too. "When I was working in Garcia, Russ came to me with a request. I said, 'Anything, son.' He said, 'You're a good uncle.' I said, 'I try to be, Russ.' He said he'd been trying to contact you. It'd been a long time since you'd spoken. He said that you didn't hate each other, that he'd met someone, finally, and I didn't know who he meant, but it was someone he felt he could have a meaningful few months with, if not longer—and then—" My brother paused, like he was taking a breath. The whole thing seemed very staged, this one-sided conversation and my taking it like a champ. "Then—what did he say? It was just that when he came to see me, he felt very bad about it. He was close to you, but he felt a kinship to me that—I didn't mean it like that, only that—do you know how hard this is for me to do? To tell you all this shit?"

"I understand."

"The hell you understand."

"I hear what you're saying."

"But now you've heard it, and that makes some kind of difference, doesn't it?"

The day before the execution, my ex-wife called to tell me she'd be wearing her earplugs. She didn't want to hear the man drowning. Probably, she told me, I'd let him up by accident, and he would plead for his life, and then one of the officers would have to do it.

"Have you ever had faith in me before?"

"If I'm being polite," she said.

"Do you think I'd have made a good dog owner?"

"Thinking about getting a dog?"

"No, I was just wondering. Been wondering a lot about how to move past everything. I think the anticipation is making it harder."

"What on earth are we talking about? Dogs? Back on topic. Drown the hell out of him. Drown him like you mean it," she said. "That's what we're talking about. Don't fuck this up."

But I didn't know how to drown anyone like I meant it.

"I wish they'd just let me shoot him or something."

"If you can't do this, then I don't know why I even bother talking to you."

I arrived at the path leading to the river and was brought through the woods by car. An SUV could have made it through the path fine; the car, however, struggled through holes and red-clay mud pools. The officer accompanying me drove silently with his head down, hoping to avoid the tree limbs that reached out at the windshield.

There were several people I knew at the river standing together in a semicircle. My brother was there: he had his hands in his pockets, exhaled warm puffs of air. My ex-wife smoked a cigarette. Her hair was poofed up in the front. They stood in front of the river, and I spoke a few words about my feelings. But they were more about myself than my son: I felt bad. I finished my brief statement, which I'd sporadically written the night before. It was never meant to be a climactic point of interest for me. I was about to kill someone—that was too far at the front of my mind for an impact statement. Ellis was obscured by those present, but the officer accompanying me asked them to make way so I could go down to the river.

Ellis stood in the water, accompanied by a guard. The guard held him at the waist by a small chain.

Ellis was much smaller than I imagined. He appeared to be a different kind of person altogether. It was very cold on top of that, and he and the guard must have felt miserable, though one of them more so than the other.

Stepping into the river, I imagined what it must have been like to be my son stepping into the water to take a bath moments before his death. This wasn't the same water, but it was the same anyway. It was cold, and I wanted to go home, and I thought of the possum, and the guard reached out his hand—

I might, supposedly, have been expected to imagine my son as a child, sitting in a bathtub, moments before me or my now-ex-wife came in to help him bathe, his skin afraid of being wet—he always fought in the tub with us, and I wondered if he'd fought there in the river.

Nervous—knowing people were watching me. A few officers, my brother, my ex-wife, two lawyers, a couple of Ellis's people—it was a whole show.

Ellis waited for me, hands behind his back. He had one of those *Mona Lisa* smiles I didn't know quite how to read, and I was so nervous I couldn't fathom interpreting a facial expression.

The guard's hand was still outstretched. "Watch your footing," he said, even though none of us were supposed to speak.

He stepped to the side of the murderer and braced himself against his shoulder. Prayer or something—that might have been useful, but as I was not allowed to speak, I could not say anything in regard to prayer.

"We were friends. I'm sorry for doing what I did," Ellis said.

I eased him into the water and held him under. The water was cold against my stomach, the pocket of emptiness between my shirt and my belly button like a packet of ice. Ellis let himself be leaned back, but the guard held on to the point of chain behind Ellis's back all the same.

There wasn't much to it—I stood there over him, one hand planted firmly against his chest to hold him down, the other wrapped against his ribs for support.

He waited patiently in the water for something. We waited for it to happen.

I wonder what he waited for—it would be a shame if people thought about death just before being executed. I didn't even know what his final meal had been. I should have asked. I didn't know anything about the man—only what I'd heard on the news and in courts and from the friend who said Ellis had a tic and was always looking around for something to be awed by. He was a stranger to me, and I didn't think that would ever change.

He looked around for some place to go. His hands were behind his back, and his feet, I could see, were shackled into place on a metal bar—he was helpless.

Eventually there was a struggle. His feet jolted in their locked position and clanked, and he splashed, and

I put my hands around his neck, squeezed, mostly for leverage—I could barely stand, we swayed, the water had splashed onto my chest. I held him under by the throat and squeezed. His neck tensed and he watched me closely through the water.

His mouth opened, dislocated itself looking for a breath of air. I looked at Ellis and the contortion of muscles and the ripples he produced. I tried to imagine what he must have thought about: he was not much different than my son.

They must have been the same people. Maybe, for instance, Ellis had a love for animals. Or maybe he collected books and had been working to better himself up until the point where everything went wrong. His eyes watched me through the water, interested, straining.

He might have been a good person five years ago, when he returned home for the first time in many years to visit his father, who'd abused him at a young age. His eyes quivered.

He might have been a good person ten years ago, when he pulled 2,000 dollars from his savings in order to help his sister through her divorce. Eventually, his eyes shut: no, they opened again, but they were blank, milky white through foggy river water, shaded.

And twelve years ago, right after dropping out of college, he had told his father that he was sorry—he couldn't do what his parents wanted anymore—he said he wanted to travel and do things on his own for a while. His father had said to him over the phone: "Don't come back here." And he didn't see his father for another seven years. A long, stupid interval of years. He was lightweight in the water like a young person.

I imagined how, twenty-four years ago, he might have been sitting on a brown-carpeted floor playing video games on a dial television, the sound of animals outside the windows, echoes chanting, a wall with years and years of thumbtack holes scattered across it like stars.

MY GRANDFATHER RAN OFF TO THE WOODS

I.

M y grandmother has been keeping my grandfather in the guest bedroom. I saw him when I went to the back of the house to use the bathroom. The door was cracked, and there he was just sitting on the side of the bed, his hands in his lap, mouth slightly open, staring at the wall perpendicular to the doorway. His skin looked splotchy and patched white in some areas. He didn't move, really, except for his chest, which shook as he breathed, like they do.

"It's good," my grandmother said. "I'm not crazy. It'll work out. Things work out, you know?"

It'd been around five years since I saw my grandfather alive, so I was a little shaken. I didn't know how these things worked.

"Well, it's been tough. But it's been good. I talk to him all the time. All the time," she said. "You can go in there and talk to him for a while. He'd probably like to see you."

I had no idea what I'd say to him, anyway.

My grandmother and I talked for a little while. Not about anything important. We talked about the furniture business. My wife and I were thinking about relocating. Some opportunities had come up, but things had been strained between the two of us lately. But I wanted to talk about my grandfather. Not about me.

I rubbed my eyes. She shook her head and said, "No, I don't know about crazy. Not that. Just lonely, lonely." She stroked the bones of her knees.

II.

My grandfather used to drink a lot of coffee. He had a big green thermos he'd drink coffee from throughout the day. He was a diabetic, and one thing I remember from when I was little was this diabetic seizure he had next to a wall at a Mexican restaurant. I was slightly embarrassed that I couldn't just go have a normal dinner with my grandparents.

I liked the meticulous lunches my grandfather would pack himself. One day, he brought a lunch box with us to Tampa so he could eat if he felt bad. He never talked a lot. But I guess that didn't matter. I miss the feeling of not knowing what to expect from anything and simultaneously not concerning yourself with whatever came along. That's childhood in a nutshell, basically.

III.

Well, the diabetes just sort of disappeared when grand-mother ordered he be dug up and stuck in her bedroom like an ornament. Now it was just a matter of grandpa being a vegetable. But sometimes he'd say something, I guess. He'd mutter "I love you" to my grandmother because she was always telling him how much she loved him. I know all this because I stood outside the bedroom while she was changing his dirty sheets. She changed his sheets every day now because, as a dead person, he always got the sheets dirty fairly quickly on account of this gross-looking black stuff he'd sweat out.

IV.

I didn't grow up with my grandparents. My grandmother would come over during the holidays and ask stupid questions like, Who cooked this? And Mom would give her a look like she knew damn well who cooked dinners during the holiday, or any day, basically.

When we were still in the business of doing family get-togethers, I was going through my phase of taking up for Mom a lot. Dad never cooked, I mean. He especially never went to see his parents, so that job fell to me because if there's one thing I hated as a teenager, it was to hear my grandmother complain to me over the phone about how sad she was that no one ever came to see her when her husband was offshore.

So I started seeing my grandparents more often when I was a teenager. Those were the years of my pre-maturity. Just moving back and forth between my parents' and grandparents' homes, until one day I met Tammy, who was a good person, owned a furniture store, and liked me, wanted to shack up for a while before getting married, and who, after a few years of us feeling what I thought was pretty happy for a relatively young couple, started acting rude with customers. She finally decided that she needed a bit of extra mental space home-wise, that this whole marriage thing needed to be put on hold for just a little while so she could clear her head, and that I should just go stay with my grandma for a little while because she was so old she could barely care for herself, much less a rotting husband who was likely to make the whole loneliness issue worse.

So that's basically how I ended up at my grandparents' house.

V.

My grandmother had a pinched nerve in her back, so she complained about everything. My grandfather didn't have feeling in any of his limbs as far as I was concerned, but he moaned a lot during the day like he needed attention.

I heard him say my grandmother's name a few times. Sometimes he asked who that was in the other room. I was sleeping on the couch, so I could hear him moaning all night. I don't think he actually slept. My grandmother would knock on his door at night and poke her head in, and I'd hear her ask how he was doing. He'd moan something back at her, and she'd ask him if he wanted some water. I don't know what else he was capable of ingesting since my grandmother was the one feeding him, and she told me not ever to worry about it because he ate early in the morning when she was up and not at all during the day. Then my grandmother would poke her head into the living room in the dark, and she'd ask if I needed anything, like I hadn't been trying to sleep either. I'd just pretend to be asleep so I wouldn't have to tell her to go away and leave me alone.

I wanted to go in there and set my grandpa on fire, put him out of his misery if only to stop all the moaning he would do.

Things get better, of course. Not much to say in the way of making things better, except that you just get used to being around certain things, certain people, and you start ignoring the moaning, imagining him standing over you in the dark, and you finally drift off to sleep, happy that your grandmother has finally decided to give up on poking her head into the living room in the dark.

VI.

When my grandma would go in there and change his sheets and give him a new pair of underwear, smells would come wafting out in thick plumes like smoke.

"You ever give him a bath?"

"It's real hard to bathe him. His skin is real bad."

"Oh," I said.

So I finally worked up the nerve to go in there and fight the stench of my grandfather. He looked at me like he didn't recognize me. I reminded him who I was and told him I was just across the hall if he ever needed anything. I said this because I was trying to be nice, and I'd rather get up and help my grandfather do whatever at night than my grandmother, who'd complain about her pinched nerve and this pain in her knees on the way back to her room, which frankly was worse than the moaning.

One night I heard papers hitting the wall. I went into the bedroom and watched him sitting there on the edge of the bed, looking through some magazine. He'd managed to get the lamp on somehow.

The magazine was an old issue of *Guns and Ammo* and had belonged to my uncle. I asked my grandfather what he was doing, and he said he was looking for a picture of himself when he was in school.

"You need a yearbook. I'll look for your yearbook tomorrow," I said.

He dropped the magazine on the floor. He moaned something incomprehensible.

"What? Can't hear you. What?"

He looked frustrated with me for not being able to hear him. I knew his speech wouldn't ever improve, so I didn't push him.

He said, "What happened to that woman?"

"What woman?"

"That woman. Sarah."

"I broke up with Sarah. I married Tammy. You remember Tammy, don't you? We went to college together. I showed you her picture a while back."

He kicked the magazine at me.

"Where's Beth?"

So I went to my grandmother's room, woke her up, and told her to go in there and do the sheets. I think she'd prepared herself for an uninterrupted rest. She was curled around a body pillow like a chimp. I, on the other hand, had proven useless in the face of helping my grandfather with the mundane task of keeping him comfortable. This is how I thought it might be for a while, a sort of back and forth between the three of us, and me trying to make myself useful now that there wasn't much else for me to do.

VII.

I didn't really notice the coyotes until my grandmother came and woke me up and told me that something weird was going on with my grandpa.

He'd gotten out of bed, apparently, and went outside sniffing for the coyotes. Flashlights in hand, we found him in the gutter next to the neighbors' house. Some dogs were barking, and somewhere a field over we heard the family of coyotes yelping.

This yelping became a regular thing for a while, and it took a few days to learn that it was the coyotes that perked him up. One night my grandmother and I were sitting in the living room when the coyote yelping started, and grandpa bounded through the living room on all fours in just his boxers.

I didn't like the feel of his oyster-like skin, so I might have let him slip out of my grasp intentionally. My grandmother fussed at me for a moment before bending over and rubbing her knees. So then I had to chase after my grandfather in the dark.

I followed the coyote yips. I shined a light across the neighbors' pasture. I walked around the fence line, looking in at the field, and eventually found my grandfather tangled up in old, loose barbed wire. This required me to go and wake the neighbors. So the neighbors went out there with wire cutters and helped me untangle my grandfather. Then they told me they'd call the cops if he ended up on their property again.

My grandmother and I had a sit-down the next day to try and decide what to do about my grandfather's obsession with the coyotes.

"Well, I could try to shoot them or something. It's not too hard to shoot at a coyote."

"Maybe if you kill one, they'll all decide to leave," she agreed.

"I guess that's how they work."

"Well, no. No, that won't work. There are too many houses around. I'd rather you not shoot the coyotes.

They didn't really do anything anyway. They're just being coyotes. Well."

So we decided that I shouldn't go and shoot at the coyotes. In the meantime we had to get a length of chain to restrain my grandpa at night. I bought two pairs of handcuffs from the adult movie store and fashioned both pairs to either side of the length of chain, which I then attached to the bed frame.

The length of chain was a good idea because when grandpa crawled out of the bed and began to make for the door, he was caught at the ankle and couldn't go any further. He tried for the window as well, but the chain prevented him from going anywhere. It was funny and sad, and I didn't know exactly what to do with myself, seeing him chained at the ankle like that, moaning and clawing, unable to speak.

My grandma suggested we just leave the chain on him throughout the day so we'd never make the mistake of getting it on him too late at night. The coyotes didn't have a regular schedule, so this seemed like a pretty good idea.

But after a few days of leaving him chained up like this, I decided his skin had some kind of allergic reaction to the cuffs. His ankles became brittle and black. There was a gnarled impression where he'd pulled all night, listening to the yelping. I think he might have tried chewing through the bone. So I decided to get rid of the chains. My grandmother was so angry and confused about this that she retreated to her bedroom and lay on her side reading the newspaper for like three hours.

VIII.

I boarded up grandpa's window, for one. I made sure he wouldn't be able to get through the plywood no matter how hard he threw himself into it. He watched me hammering at the wall as he rubbed his ankle. I became conscious of his heavy breathing again and felt him watching me during the day a lot of the time, and I knew this wasn't because he hated me or wanted me out of his life but because he knew I was trying to keep him from something he for whatever reason thought he needed to protect us from. Then I wondered if that's what was going on with his arousal at the sound of coyotes—protecting us? I don't know. Probably not.

They came that night. We had the door to his room bolted. I sat up in the living room, listening to his body flinging against the plywood window. Then he started pounding against the door. Grandma jumped at every sound.

"We'll think of something else," I said.

She shook her head. I think she was too worried to say or do anything. This is a lot like what I was like when I was going through mine and Tammy's separation—too sad and worried to really talk about it or try to fix things. So it is.

IX.

I think it was that she was mostly afraid of dying herself. I hesitated for a while to ask her about what exactly she wanted after she died. She told me to just let her stay in the ground. She didn't want to be a burden to me or my family anyway.

"There are places you could go. I could work something out though. You know, people who could help you out and stuff."

She didn't say anything for a while. She made coffee. Neither of us had gotten any sleep for a few nights. One night the coyotes wouldn't come, and we'd sleep a little, but our bodies and minds had adjusted to this sudden consistent lack of sleep, and we'd wake in the middle of the night with Grandpa in mind, go in there, and put our ears up to the door and listen.

She lay on her side, reading the paper. I stood in the doorway, scratching my elbows.

She said, "No. Don't bother with me. It's not really something I want to talk about anyway."

X.

The pounding on the door some nights was not him but just some thing that existed in the world that had no relation to us. Grandma even told me one day that he was starting to behave like a wild animal. She began to take pills. She'd throw up around four in the afternoon some kind of milky green stuff. I asked her if she needed to go to the doctor, and she kept saying, "No, no, it's nothing, just old-person sickness." I talked to Tammy about it, and Tammy asked me what exactly my problem was—couldn't I take care of an old woman?

"I don't have a problem. My problem is I want to come home. But I have to hear from you every now and then if I'm ever going to come home."

"Well, what if I say 'come home'? Then you'll leave Beth. And if you leave Beth then she'll poison herself to death."

I really didn't like the idea of being the one thing keeping my grandmother from committing suicide. But the way Tammy saw it was that it was a lucky thing she'd kicked me out of the house when she did. I told her about the coyotes, though, and my grandpa acting up at night.

"Crunch up some poison and put it in meat," she said. "That's about what it takes. But then again I don't know if poison'll take down a coyote. Poison is for rats and stuff, right?"

"It's an idea," I said. "Where do I get poison?"

"The poison store. I don't know?"

In the other room my grandfather moaned something about wanting coffee. I heard my grandmother go in there and ask him to repeat himself, and then he said something about wanting his insulin shot.

"Look, it's just insane here. I just want to work things out. Can't we work things out?"

"You told me that I could fuck myself, so here we are," she said. "Remember? 'Go fuck yourself,' you said. How do you say that to someone who's going through major withdrawals? You know how serious my withdrawals are?"

"I don't know what to say. I'm sorry."

"Now you're sorry."

"Yes."

"I'm sorry," she said.

XI.

That night my grandfather hurled himself into the plywood so hard that his neck snapped. I could hear the bone crunching from my bedroom. I went in there and helped him back into bed. He rubbed at his head and moaned. Coyotes were growling in the field next to us. I wondered if they were chasing the cattle. Then I wondered why the hell the neighbors weren't doing something about the coyotes since it was their field the predators were prowling. I planned to call them the next day. I'd fix their fence and work things out.

Grandpa took my hands and put them on his neck and rolled his head a little like he needed help reconnecting himself.

"I can't," I said. I really couldn't. His skin felt like raw oysters.

Then I noticed the huge gash on top of his head.

I pressed his body into the mattress and covered him up. The coyotes were howling out in the field. He started shaking, panting wildly. I turned the lamp off.

XII.

Nights like this didn't go on for much longer.

I called the neighbors, apologized again, and asked why the hell they hadn't done something about the coyotes that'd been chasing their cattle.

"Not chasing the cattle," they said. "Rabbits probably. Cows are fine. Coyotes aren't hurting anything."

"I'll come over and fix the fence. I bought a roll of wire. I'll come over pretty soon."

"Thank you," they said. They didn't seem like such bad people, really.

We didn't have poison, and I didn't want to ask anyone whether poison would actually kill a coyote, so I kept my mouth shut about it. What we had was an old window that'd been taken out of the shed when they had to rebuild it after a hurricane. My grandmother was keeping the window for some reason I didn't know—it's just the way old people are.

I'm sure my grandmother would have detested my idea of crunching up a bunch of glass with a hammer and rolling it in a few pounds of meat. I read about this somewhere. I twined a few lengths of barbed wire together, discarded the rest, looked around to make sure no one was watching, and took the meat out of a sack I'd brought. I hurled it out into the field, and that was that. I know it's a horrible thing to do to an animal.

XIII.

But it doesn't matter because the meat didn't work. The coyotes came back three nights later. I went out to the neighbors' fence and looked out at them with a flashlight. The pack was barely noticeable and looked like so many little blots moving through the thistle and cogon grass. I considered just letting it go and staying the night in a hotel room.

Grandma was sitting in the living room smoking a cigarette when I got back.

She said, "Don't look at me like that. Don't act like I can't be goofy for a little bit."

I took a cigarette from the pack and sniffed it.

"When I was in college I smoked a little. We weren't supposed to smoke in the dormitory," she said. "So we'd go out on the balcony with a wet rag and spin the rag around in the air and smoke." She spun this little pillow around to demonstrate, and it flew across the living room and landed by the television.

I smoked like two puffs and decided I didn't want anymore. It sat in an ashtray the rest of the night.

"I used to sit up and watch television all night," she said. "Before I got your granddaddy back, I mean, that's all I'd do all night. Then I'd sleep all day. Looks like it'll be back to that soon. I don't think I can stand it much longer."

She'd stopped jumping at the sound of his banging against the door and window. We talked about our futures. She thought she'd be dead soon. She reminded me again that what she wanted was to just be buried in the ground, undisturbed, for as long as it would take. Then she told me just how much reanimating my grandfather had set her back. "Don't worry—you've got insurance money coming your way. I'm worth something. Only thing is, you can't reanimate me if you claim the money. So there's that."

I thought, well, this whole thing is selfish. Why don't we just talk about keeping her in the ground when she's such a hypocrite? With my grandfather in there killing himself again trying to get out into the world? I told her this. I used my harsh voice. She drew back in her chair. Then she reminded me that she'd do anything to defeat the feeling of being a widow.

"It'll happen again," I said, meaning she'd be a widow soon. "That's what it's worth. You know?"

She didn't say anything. She closed her eyes. Then she shook her head, got up, and went to read her paper in the bed.

XIV.

I had to speak to my grandfather first before taking him out for a ride. He sat up carefully in bed when I came in. I turned the lamp on, and he put his hands on the side of the bed. His chest heaved in and out. I told myself his body wasn't a healthy thing that could go on much longer.

"Why do you want to get out so bad? You know, when the coyotes start barking or whatever?"

He looked at the floor, shook his head, and sighed.

"Are you bored? Is that it? Are you bored?"

I'd tried asking him this before, of course. He always sighed. Sometimes he asked for Beth. Then sometimes he'd rub his purpled face or touch his bruised shoulders or finger the gash on top of his head. His body was deteriorating at an exponential rate. I knelt next to his bed now and touched his skin. He let me touch his skin and he started to rub his face.

"Look, do you want to go? How bad do you want to get out?"

His face was crooked. Lately, there'd be some sort of uncanny growth I can't begin to explain—like he was bloating, which might have been a side effect of all the slamming into doors and plywood windows.

"You hear me, don't you?" I snapped my fingers in his ear.

His mouth drooped slightly, but he didn't attempt to communicate.

Then for whatever reason I started talking about Tammy. It was something about how I wished we could just get along. Like, I had no clue really what to say about the situation. "She just doesn't know how to articulate her feelings," I said. Which I don't think is what I really meant. What I think I meant is that she didn't love me. Or that she thought I was supposed to be someone else. I was thinning on the top and my teeth were crooked.

"How did you do it?" I asked. "When you and Grandma had fallings out? What did you do about it?"

He shrugged his shoulders. It was the best form of communication. And I guess it said to me that he really didn't remember how marriage was supposed to work.

"You don't know. I'll take that. I guess. It's just hard. I don't think you're proud of me though. You remember meeting Tammy that one time? She came in and stood next to the bed, and you talked about where she was from. You said she was pretty. I guess you thought she was pretty."

Grandpa looked at me. Looked like he was embarrassed of the angular droop of his mouth.

"Well, anyway," I said. I told him to come on and get up. I helped him up and led him out of the room. The coyotes hadn't started growling or yelping yet. We went out on the porch. To the left, in the window, a light shined, and my grandmother lay on the bed, probably reading a paper.

I put him in the car and told him to buckle up. Which he didn't do. He was wearing his boxers and looked pitiful and anxious sitting next to me.

He watched me as I drove. A gravel road came up, and I coasted with the windows down until he started looking around sporadically. Then I parked, unsure exactly where we were.

He started shaking, twirling his arms violently, then fought with the door. I was too afraid to stop him as he jumped from the car and loped to the front into the headlights. Something yelped out into the dark. I yelled at him, unbuckled, and started to get out, my hands slick, my chest a solid mass of hot wooden fear. He got down on all fours and bounded off into the woods. He didn't turn back and look at me. I sat in the gravel in the dark for a while and listened to the coyotes. They cried and wept, and the moon hung over the line in the trees where the road led out into the thick country woods.

ACKNOWLEDGMENTS

I want to thank Joanna Ashley for the years of support and for helping me get through the first draft of almost everything I've written. If it weren't for her, I might not have broken through.

I also want to thank the constant readers and supporters I've had over the years: Micah Dean Hicks, Ellis Purdie, Nickalus Rupert, Apoorva Bradshaw-Mittal, Micah-Jade Coleman, Daniel J. Pinney, Brenda Peynado, Luis Iglesias, Mary Ann Avallone O'Gorman, Eddie Malone, Tom Holmes, Tracie Dawson, Michael Czyzniejewski, Jordan James, Bryana Fern, Dustin Hoffman, Jonathan and Danielle Kelly, Jay Digel, Matthew Arnold, Patrick Lambert, and Nick Travis.

The amazing faculty that helped my writing at the University of Southern Mississippi: Anne Sanow, Olivia Clare Friedman, Andrew Milward, Joshua Bernstein, and Steve Barthelme, who always pushed me to be better. I'm also grateful for Adaku Ankumah for telling me to focus on my writing my first year at Tuskegee University.

I appreciate Sheila Williams and Trevor Quachri for giving me a space in their magazines. I wonder if editors really know how much it means to writers when they finally make it in.

Thank you to Kevin Morgan Watson and Claire Foxx for giving this collection of stories a chance—I'll never forget this.

Finally, thank you to my family for their belief in my work: Mom and Dad, Grandparents, and everyone I talked with on the phone through the pandemic. I miss everyone.

◆◆◆

Thank you also to the editors and literary magazines that first published these stories, sometimes in slightly different forms:

Asimov's Science Fiction: "Brother Swine," "Skin," and "Riding the Waves of Leviathan"

DIAGRAM: "Beautiful Bird"

Red Rock Review: "Movements" and "My Grandfather Ran off to the Woods"

Sonora Review: "Periphylla, and Other Deep Ocean Attractions"

Yemassee: "Last Stand of the Alligator Killers"

GARRETT ASHLEY

has lived most of his life in Mississippi, and at the beginning of the pandemic he finished his Ph.D. at the University of Southern Mississippi's Center for Writers. His work has appeared in *Asimov's Science Fiction*, *The Normal School*, *Sonora Review*, *Analog SF&F*, *DIAGRAM*, *Reed Magazine*, and *Sequestrum*, among other places. His story collection *Before the Snakes Came* was recently a finalist for the 2022 Moon City Press Short Fiction Award. *Periphylla, and Other Deep Ocean Attractions* is his debut story collection and was named Runner-Up for the 2023 Press 53 Award for Short Fiction.